P9-CAJ-895

Here's what teens are saying about Bluford High:

"I love the Bluford series because I can relate to the stories and the characters. They are just like real life. Ever since I read the first one, I've been hooked."
—*Jolene P.*

"All the Bluford books are great. There wasn't one that I didn't like, and I read them all—twice!"
—*Sequoyah D.*

"I found it very easy to lose myself in these books. They kept my interest from beginning to end and were always realistic. The characters are vivid, and the endings left me in eager anticipation of the next book."
—*Keziah J.*

"As soon as I finished one book, I couldn't wait to start the next one. No books have ever made me do that before."
—*Terrance W.*

"Each Bluford book gives you a story that could happen to anyone. The details make you feel like you are inside the books. The storylines are amazing and realistic. I loved them all."
—*Elpiclio B.*

"Man! These books are amazing!"
—*Dominique J.*

BLUFORD HIGH

The Test

PEGGY KERN

Series Editor: Paul Langan

SCHOLASTIC INC.

ISBN 978-0-545-39552-6

12 11 10 9 8 7 6 5 4 3 2 1   13 14 15 16 17 18/0

Printed in the U.S.A.   23

First Scholastic printing, February 2013

Chapter 1

Liselle Mason stared into the cracked mirror of the Bluford High School girls' bathroom. She had been standing there for several minutes, fussing with her hair and trying to cover up the dark rings under her eyes with makeup. There was a stain on her jeans, and her white shirt was slightly wrinkled. She pulled on the front of it, hoping the wrinkles would disappear.

Give it up, girl, she told herself with a sigh. *You're a mess.*

She checked her watch. It was 11:30 a.m. In ten minutes she would be standing in front of a group of teenage girls in Bluford's library. Her stomach flipped nervously every time she thought about it. She had never talked to a large group of people before. But when Ms. Spencer,

1

Bluford's principal, called her a few weeks ago, Liselle felt she couldn't say no. Not after all that had happened.

"*Liselle, I think it would be very helpful for the students to hear your story,*" Ms. Spencer had said. "*I'd like you to be the guest speaker at a small assembly I'm having for some of Bluford's female students. I know it might be difficult, but would you be willing to share your story with the girls here?*"

"*I don't know, Ms. Spencer,*" Liselle had replied nervously. Just hearing her old principal's voice again brought back a wave of painful memories. "*I mean, I don't know what I could tell them. I'm no kind of role model. You of all people should know that.*"

Ms. Spencer had been quiet for a moment, as if she was searching for the right words. "*You can tell them the truth, Liselle,*" she finally replied. "Your *truth. That's all I'm asking.*"

It had been four years since Liselle had set foot in Bluford High School. She was twenty years old now, and yet she couldn't help but feel like a sixteen-year-old again as she looked around the bathroom. She clearly remembered the blue-and-white checkered tile on the floor, the shiny gray paint on the walls, the echoing of footsteps in the hallway outside. Liselle walked over to the last stall and opened the door. She closed her eyes tight against the memory of what had happened to her there.

I never thought I'd be back here, she thought. *But here I am.*

Liselle took one last look at herself in the mirror. *Get it together, girl*, she thought. *Don't get nervous now. They're just a bunch of kids, right?* Then she walked out into the hallway and down the long, silent corridor.

Ms. Spencer was waiting just outside the library door.

"Hello, Liselle," she said with a warm smile. "Thank you for coming. You look so mature. Not like the young kid I remember."

"Thanks," said Liselle, trying to straighten the front of her shirt again. "It's been a long time. Sorry I'm such a mess. It was a crazy morning."

Ms. Spencer put a reassuring hand on Liselle's shoulder. "You look just fine. I know you have your hands full these days, and I appreciate you finding the time to do this. Are you ready? The students are waiting for you."

Liselle peeked into the library window. "I think so," she replied nervously. "It's just . . . I'm still not sure what to say to them."

"Just start at the beginning, Liselle. Take your time. I should warn you, some of these girls are more . . . challenging . . . than others. But I'll be right there with you, in case we have any problems."

Liselle followed Ms. Spencer into the library. About thirty students were spread out across the room, sitting at tables or in small clusters on the carpeted floor. They were all wearing bright yellow stickers with their names written in black magic marker. Some were waiting quietly, thumbing through their notebooks and fiddling with their pens. Others talked to their friends and shifted impatiently in their seats.

Liselle recognized Jamee Wills, who lived not far from her apartment. Jamee looked surprised to see her there.

"Hey Jamee," she whispered with a smile. Jamee smiled quickly and looked away, as if she didn't want her classmates to realize they knew each other.

"Yo, Ms. Spencer, when you gonna tell us what we're here for?" shouted a

4

girl from the back of the room. She was wearing a tight-fitting red T-shirt, dark blue jeans and red lipstick. Her hair was long and brown and arranged into neat thin braids. Her name tag said "Tamara."

"Yeah, Ms. Spencer! Why you being all mysterious about it? We in trouble or something?" added another girl who was sitting at the table with Tamara. She too was wearing a snug shirt with a red rhinestone heart in the middle.

"You're about to find out, April," Ms. Spencer answered. "This is Liselle Mason. She used to be a student here at Bluford. Today she's going to talk to you about a very important topic, and I expect you girls to listen carefully and be respectful."

Tamara and April groaned. "Man, I thought we were going to watch a movie or something," said April. She was chewing a large wad of gum and leaning back in her chair, twirling a long piece of black hair around her slender finger.

Tamara eyed Liselle suspiciously. "Whatever," she added. "I don't care what this girl has to say. How long we gotta sit here?"

"That's enough!" said Ms. Spencer

firmly. "If you can't sit quietly and listen, you can head straight to my office."

Liselle smiled knowingly as she watched the two girls. "I got this, Ms. Spencer," she said with a sudden burst of energy, striding up to the front of the room. "My name's Liselle, and like Ms. Spencer said, I used to go to school here."

"*So?*" snapped Tamara. A few of the other students giggled. Jamee shot them an annoyed glare.

"Can you just let her talk?" Jamee grumbled.

"It's okay, Jamee," Liselle replied calmly.

Tamara looked Liselle over with a critical eye. "Figures you two know each other," she laughed. "Man, look at her jeans! All stained and nasty!" Laughter rippled through the room.

Liselle put a hand on her hip and smiled calmly. "So, you're the tough girl, huh? How old are you?"

"Sixteen," Tamara answered defiantly. "How old are *you?*"

Liselle continued, ignoring her question. "I bet you're *real* popular, too. I bet nobody messes with you."

"That's right," Tamara said proudly, crossing her arms. "And?"

6

Liselle looked around the library thoughtfully. "You know, in all my years at Bluford High, I don't think I was ever in this room. My friends and I used to make fun of the kids who studied in here. We thought they were losers."

"Look who's talkin'," Tamara mumbled. The comment was aimed at Tamara's friends, but Liselle heard it.

She smiled and nodded at Tamara. "I probably look old to you, huh?" Liselle said. "I bet you think we don't have anything in common. Maybe you won't believe this, but when I was your age, *I* was the tough girl. Right, Ms. Spencer?"

"It's true," nodded the principal.

"I spent a lot of time in Ms. Spencer's office. I remember this one time, my friends put a lit cigarette under the smoke detector in the girl's bathroom. The alarm went off and the entire school was evacuated."

Several students snickered. A few, who hadn't been paying much attention, suddenly looked up.

Tamara smirked and arched an eyebrow. "So? That was like years ago. You don't look so popular now."

"No. I guess I don't," said Liselle with a shrug. "I used to think my whole life

7

would be as easy as it was when I was sixteen. I wouldn't have to work hard. I didn't even have to go to class if I didn't want to. I thought I'd be young forever. My friends would always be there. And no matter what happened, someone would be there to fix it for me."

Liselle sat down in a chair at the front of the room and rubbed her forehead. She could feel a dull ache building behind her tired eyes. She laughed bitterly and shook her head. "I actually believed we'd be together, me and Oscar."

Tamara picked at her nails. She looked bored. "Ain't my fault if you can't keep a man," she murmured, quietly enough so that Ms. Spencer couldn't hear. Then she pulled out a small red cell phone from her backpack and began texting under the table.

"That's cold," someone said.

For a moment, Liselle's face burned with anger. She could feel the entire room watching her, waiting to see how she would respond. She imagined herself striding over to Tamara and kicking the chair right out from underneath her. That's what she would have done four years ago, when she was Tamara's age.

Liselle stood up and walked over to

Tamara's table, her face serious but also slightly amused. She leaned in close to Tamara, who suddenly looked surprised. Tamara glanced at Ms. Spencer, then at April, who was staring at the floor.

"I'd be offended by what you just said to me," Liselle said firmly, "if I thought you had any idea what you were talking about." She then took the cell phone from Tamara's hand and slipped it into her pocket.

"Hey, that's mine. You can't take that—"

"I don't care what you think about me," Liselle cut her off, locking her eyes on Tamara. "But for the next hour, you're *gonna* listen to what I gotta say. Understand? So sit up straight, girl. Pay attention. And quit pickin' at your nails. You might just learn something. You'll get your phone back when I'm done."

"Oh snap!" someone said.

"She just schooled you, Tamara!" another girl added.

A wave of excitement rippled through the room. Liselle walked back to her chair at the front of the room.

"Look," she said, staring into each of the faces in front of her. "I'm not here to lecture you. And some of you might not

9

wanna hear what I have to say. But here it is."

Liselle took a deep breath and glanced at Ms. Spencer. "When I was sixteen, I got pregnant."

For a moment, the room went quiet. A girl sitting next to Jamee, whose nametag said "Cindy," dropped her pen. April shifted in her seat and looked at the door, as if she wanted to run out of the room. But other students, including Tamara, rolled their eyes as if they had heard this story before.

"Here we go," grumbled Tamara, shaking her head. "Now we know why she's here."

"My cousin had a baby last month. He's soooo cute!" blurted a short, round-faced girl.

"Danisha, don't no one wanna hear 'bout your cousin's kid," said a girl wearing a yellow shirt. Her nametag said "Nyeema."

"I'm just sayin'," Danisha protested. "Babies are cute."

"Well, my sister had a baby last year," Nyeema added. "All he does is cry and poop. That ain't cute. That's just nasty, and I'm the one who does all the babysitting."

"How old is your sister?" Liselle asked.

"Eighteen," Nyeema answered.

Liselle nodded and glanced at Ms. Spencer.

"Eighteen ain't *that* young," snapped Tamara. "That's how old my momma was when she had me. I bet lots of girls in this room have moms who were young when they had them. And we turnin' out all right."

"C'mon, girl," April murmured. "You know what she's tryin' to say."

"Excuse me?" Tamara replied, staring at her friend. "What, you all interested now?"

April crossed her arms and looked away.

"My mom was young, too," Liselle continued. "And I'm not here to judge anyone. But I wonder, how many of you really understand what it's like to have a child? I mean, *really* understand?"

"I do," said Nyeema. "Screamin' and cryin'. That's all they do."

"Not my cousin's baby," added Danisha.

"Girl, would you stop," snapped Nyeema. "The kid ain't a doll."

"What do you know?"

11

"More than you! You ever change a diaper or clean spit-up?"

The two went back and forth, and for a second Liselle wondered if she had made a mistake. She was about to break up the argument, when April leaned forward in her seat.

"So, what happened with you?" she asked quietly.

Tamara shook her head and rolled her eyes, but she didn't say a word. The two girls behind her stopped arguing. A hush spread across the library.

Liselle felt eyes turn toward her. She looked out at the young faces. For a moment, she thought she saw a girl sitting alone in the corner, her hair in short, tight cornrows, her arms crossed self-consciously over her baggy T-shirt. She could have sworn she saw herself as she rose from her chair.

"I'm not proud of the story I'm about to tell you," Liselle began. "There are certain things that happened—things that I'm ashamed of. I made some really bad choices."

Liselle looked away for a moment, her eyes burning with tears she refused to let fall.

"But I got hurt, too. Hurt like I never

thought I could be. In the end, you gotta make your own choices. But maybe you can learn from my mistakes. That's why I'm here. Everybody's different. And I don't know how it is for other girls who've faced the same situation."

"All I can tell you," continued Liselle, "is how it was for me."

Chapter 2

Four years earlier . . .

Bang! Bang! Bang!

Liselle Mason winced. She sat alone on the cold tile floor of the girl's bathroom at Bluford High School. It was almost 4:00 on Friday afternoon. Most of the students had gone home. She knew Monique Reese, her best friend, was waiting for her in the SuperFoods parking lot just down the street. If she stayed much longer, Monique would wonder where she was.

"Hello?" a female voice yelled from the hallway. Liselle didn't recognize it. "Is anyone in there?"

Go away, Liselle whispered to herself.

Her hands shook and beads of sweat gathered on her forehead. Her backpack was crumpled on the floor next to her. She laid her head on it, staring at the blue-and-white checkered tile. She wished she could just go to sleep and forget everything.

Since it was so late in the day, Liselle figured no one would come up to the remote third-floor bathroom. She had even pushed the heavy metal trash can in front of the door just in case, and then she locked herself in the last stall.

Clenched in her right hand was the long white plastic strip. Next to her was the white box. "Clear and Easy Pregnancy Test. Results in Five Minutes!" said the words in bold pink letters.

Has it been five minutes? she wondered.

She felt as if she had been sitting there for much longer. But each time she began to unclench her fist and look at the test, her heart would hammer in her chest like a furious drum.

"Just get it over with," she mumbled when she couldn't take it anymore.

Liselle sat up and yanked the cap off. Then she examined the tiny window. For a moment, she had trouble focusing her eyes. But then, from out of the stark whiteness, a blue plus sign appeared. It seeped into the soft material underneath the plastic, like blood spreading from a wound. Slowly, it grew darker and darker.

"Hello?" the voice yelled again.

Liselle cringed and shoved the cap back on.

"Go *away!*" she shouted.

The voice was young, too young to be a teacher's. *It's probably one of those kids who stay late for cheerleading or some other stupid club,* Liselle thought bitterly. Her ears were ringing, and a wave of nausea rose up in her stomach. She tried to think.

When was my last period? It's January now. November, maybe? October? She wasn't sure exactly, but it had been more than a couple of months. Liselle had tried to ignore this fact, figuring it would return as it had every month since she was twelve years old. But weeks had passed and her period never came. Then she noticed her jeans were getting snug around the waist. This morning, she couldn't even fit into her favorite pair.

Please, no, she thought looking at her face in the mirror before she left. *Were her cheeks fuller too?* she wondered. *Don't let it be that.*

On her way to school, she had stopped in SuperFoods and walked down aisle seven, pulling the hood from her jacket over her head and turning up the music in her headphones. Then she had grabbed the same pregnancy test her cousin Shayna had taken last year. She remembered it because of the pink exclamation mark after the words "Results in Five Minutes!"

She had wanted to slip the box into her backpack and walk out without facing the cashier. But the store manager lingered at the end of the aisle fiddling with bottles of cough medicine. Liselle was sure he was watching her, so she paid for the test with a crumpled twenty-dollar bill she had taken from the tip jar in Mom's bedroom. Then she buried the small white box in her backpack and rushed out.

All day she had waited, pretending everything was fine, ignoring the dizziness she felt from time to time, especially when she stood up from her desk after class. When the final bell rang, she lingered anxiously at her locker until the hallways emptied out. Then she snuck into the third-floor bathroom, careful to make sure no one was following her.

She had told Monique that Mr. Mitchell, her English teacher, was making her stay after school to complete a missing homework assignment. She knew Monique would believe her. She was often kept late by one teacher or another.

But now what? she wondered, her hands cold and trembling. She hadn't told anyone of her suspicions, not Monique, not Oscar, and especially not Mom. The thought of Mom finding out made her cringe.

It has to be wrong, Liselle told herself. She popped off the cap of the test and studied it again. The plus sign was dark blue now, the color of a bruise.

No, she thought, her hands trembling. *It can't be right. I can't be pregnant.* She reread the directions on the back of the box: "A blue plus sign indicates pregnancy. 99% accurate results!"

The words taunted her. "*This test is never wrong!*" they seemed to say, "*You're pregnant, girl. So whatcha gonna do now?!*"

Outside her stall, the metal trash can scraped along the bathroom floor. Someone was pushing hard against the door.

"Hello?" the voice said again. "Anyone

18

in here?"

"Just gimme a minute!" Liselle shouted angrily. She could feel her pulse throbbing in her forehead. She felt foggy and confused, as if she had been startled from a deep sleep.

It can't be, she told herself again and again. *I mean, wouldn't I know if I was pregnant? I don't feel any different. Shayna threw up almost every day when she was pregnant with Ruby. I don't feel sick at all.*

"Hello?" the voice cut in. This time it was closer.

Why doesn't this girl just leave me alone?

"Just gimme a minute," Liselle repeated, louder than before.

Footsteps echoed on the floor, then stopped. Liselle stood up, rubbing her eyes. She felt cornered—and angry at the person who was now standing on the other side of the door.

"You all right in there?"

Liselle snapped. She stormed from the stall and bumped into the girl standing outside. Instantly Liselle recognized her face. It was Kendra, a senior at Bluford High.

"What's your problem?" Liselle huffed.

"I told you to *wait*. Are you deaf or something?"

As she spoke, she realized she still held the pregnancy test in her hand. Quickly, she shoved it into the pocket of her sweatshirt. Then she noticed the empty white box. It still rested on the floor next to her backpack. The words on the outside seemed like a giant billboard.

Results in five minutes!

Kendra stared at them. "Oh," she said, stepping back, her eyes focused downward.

Liselle felt horrified. She dropped to her knees and grabbed the box, shoving it deep into her backpack.

"This ain't none of your business," Liselle barked as she stood up and stepped out of the stall. "You didn't see nothin', y'hear me?" Her body trembled with anger and embarrassment.

"Don't worry about me right now," Kendra finally said, her voice surprisingly gentle. "I'm not gonna tell anybody anything."

Liselle sighed. "Girl, don't lie to me. I know who you are. You're an office aide. You better not go and tell Ms. Spencer," she said, trying to hide the emotion in her voice.

"I won't," Kendra answered sincerely. "I won't even mention I saw you. I was just checking, 'cause it's 4:00, and the building is closing. You can't stay here."

Kendra was wearing a plain white button-down shirt and loose-fitting jeans. Her brown hair was pulled back into a simple ponytail. Liselle wondered what the older girl thought of her as she stood there in baggy sweatpants, hiding in the bathroom so she could take a pregnancy test. She pulled at the front of her blue T-shirt, suddenly feeling embarrassed.

"I-I know," Liselle stammered. "I was about to leave anyway, before you came barging in."

"Are you okay?" Kendra asked.

For a moment, Liselle felt like a little kid. She almost wanted to tell Kendra the truth, even though she barely knew her. She had seen her a few times in the office answering phones and filing papers. Sometimes she would show up in the parking lot of SuperFoods after school, where students often gathered to hang out. But she never stayed very long.

Kendra seemed to be smart, the kind of girl who might know what to do in this situation. *I think I might be pregnant,* Liselle imagined herself saying. She could barely think the words. *I don't know what to do.*

"Do you want me to call somebody?" Kendra continued. "I mean, if you're upset . . ."

The suggestion hit like a slap in the face. *Who am I gonna call?* she wanted to say. *How can I tell anybody about this?* Instead she glared at Kendra.

"I'm fine."

"Look," Kendra said after a moment, "I don't know you, but if you're in some kind of trouble . . ." She glanced at Liselle's hand, which was still shaking slightly. "You should tell somebody. That's all."

Liselle hoisted up her backpack.

Forget it, she thought to herself. *This girl don't know nothin'. She can't help. She ain't nothin' like me. Besides, the test is probably wrong. It's gotta be.*

Liselle wiped the smudged black eyeliner from underneath her sharp, brown eyes. Then she strode up to Kendra and jabbed a finger into her chest. Though Kendra was older, Liselle was slightly taller. She felt powerful standing in front of her. And for a second that made Liselle feel better.

"You better do what you said and keep your mouth shut," she whispered angrily as she zipped her backpack shut. "This ain't none of your business. If I find out you said a word about this to anyone . . ."

Kendra sighed and shook her head. "Whatever you say," she said, stepping away from Liselle. "I was just tryin' to help. It's 4:00 and—"

"I know. I heard you," Liselle replied angrily. "I'm outta here anyway. I hate this place."

"Liselle! Over here, girl!"

Liselle forced herself to smile as she walked toward the back parking lot of SuperFoods. A large group of students were gathered there, as they often were after school. Since it was Friday, there were even more students than usual, standing in small groups, laughing and listening to the music that pumped from several parked cars. Some were eating slices from Niko's Pizza.

Monique waved to her from across the parking lot. She was leaning up against a black Hyundai. A group of boys were standing nearby and watched Liselle as she approached her friends.

Liselle pulled her baggy gray jacket around her and walked faster.

"Yo, Liselle!" said a thin boy in a red basketball jersey. "What's up, girl? You goin' to Damian's party tomorrow night?"

Liselle's head was throbbing. She didn't feel like talking to anyone. *Just pretend that everything's normal,* she told herself.

"Not if you're gonna be there," Liselle shot back. "I ain't got time to be babysitting no little kids."

"Little kids?" he replied with a grin. "Girl, you lookin' at a man right here."

"Oh, I'm *lookin',*" Liselle continued. "But all I see is a broke-down boy who needs a haircut."

Laughter erupted from the crowd. "Oh no she *didn't,*" said another boy. "Yo, Will! She just *told* you!"

"Always does," Will chuckled. "That girl always got a comeback."

Monique called out to her then. She was wearing a short blue denim skirt and a puffy yellow jacket. Her hair was pulled back into a tight ponytail.

"Over here, girl!" she said.

The boys turned toward Monique, who tossed her head back and smiled.

"Monique, though," Will continued.

"She's *fine*."

"You *know* it," the other boy added with a smile.

Liselle looked down at her scuffed black sneakers and gray sweatpants. She was used to boys ignoring her, or losing interest once they got close enough. Her round face and straight, thick body, she thought, was built more for basketball than for the snug jeans and small skirts her friends liked to wear.

Over the summer, Monique had decided to give Liselle a "makeover." She taught her how to line her sharp brown eyes with coal-colored eyeliner and fill in her lips with lip gloss. Before a party at the end of the summer, she had even squeezed Liselle into a pair of tight-fitting jeans and a shirt that stopped just short of her waistline.

And girl, you've got to stop braidin' your hair like that, Monique had insisted. *You should grow it long. Boys like long hair.*

Liselle knew her friend meant well, but Liselle felt uncomfortable wearing Monique's outfit. She didn't like the way the boys stared at her. She felt awkward and exposed, and she was never sure if people were laughing at her. Plus, she noticed, she could barely move. And so she had gone back to her more comfortable clothing, though secretly she envied Monique's confidence. There was something about Monique that sparkled. She seemed to thrive on the attention she got from boys. Liselle felt dull in comparison. She had a hard time keeping up.

Girls like me don't get pregnant, she thought, staring at her friend.

"What took you so long? You must've really pissed off Mr. Mitchell this time," Monique said with a grin as Liselle walked up to the car. "What'd you do, anyway?"

Liselle shrugged. "Forgot my homework," she lied.

"More like you didn't do it. *Again,*" Monique replied. The hard bassline of a hip-hop song thumped from a car that was parked nearby. Monique swayed and snapped her fingers to the beat. "Ooh, I love this song!" she exclaimed.

Liselle quickly scanned the parking lot. In the distance, she saw Oscar Price sitting in the front seat of a dark blue, slightly beat-up car. His head nodded to the slow, steady beat that vibrated the car windows. Liselle stood up straight and fiddled with the edge of her jacket.

Did he see me? she wondered, hoping he would look in her direction.

Monique nudged her with an elbow. "Stop starin', girl."

"I wasn't," Liselle said quickly.

Monique shook her head and raised a suspicious eyebrow. "You still messin' with that boy?"

"Nah," Liselle replied defensively. "Not really."

Monique fished through her pocketbook. "That boy is *fine*," she said, pulling out a tube of pink lip gloss. "A lot of girls would like to get with him."

Liselle's face grew hot. She tried to choke back a wave of nausea that crept up from her stomach. In truth, she hadn't spoken to Oscar in two months. She cringed thinking of the last time they had talked. She tried to push it from her mind. But she continued to look in his direction, hoping he would smile at her or wave her over to the car or something. Anything.

Pregnant. The word stuck in her throat.

"I'm done with that boy," she said weakly.

"I'm bored," Monique sighed, leaning

back on the car and swinging her legs. "Man, I can't wait for summer. You still gonna work at the mall with me, right?"

"Yeah," Liselle answered, her voice limp. "Definitely."

Monique had a part-time job as a cashier in a clothing store. The girls planned to work there together over the summer, when the store needed extra help. Liselle had been excited about the idea of spending her summer at the mall, making extra money and hanging out with her friends. But now the future seemed foggy and far away, as if she was trying to open her eyes in a dream.

Oscar finally glanced in Liselle's direction. He smiled slightly and nodded at her, then looked away again, laughing with his friends. A dull ache throbbed against her forehead. She felt weary, as if even her bones were tired.

Please let the test be wrong, she hoped.

"You coming to Damian's party Saturday night?" asked Monique, who was still snapping her fingers and dancing.

Liselle pictured what Monique would do if she had found her in the bathroom. Monique was her closest friend, but they rarely talked about serious things. Mostly they traded gossip about classmates or boys or what movie they wanted to go see. Liselle couldn't imagine how she would respond to such an announcement.

"*I lied before, girl. I was late 'cause I snuck to the third-floor bathroom and took a pregnancy test. I'm pregnant.*" Just thinking about the words made Liselle's stomach turn.

So instead she said nothing, but her mind kept churning.

What would Oscar say? And what about Mom?

Liselle closed her eyes and tried to push the thoughts away. She had hoped seeing her friend would help her forget what happened. But the more she tried to clear her head, the louder Monique's voice seemed, and the laughter of other kids seemed to grow. And the music started to annoy her. And Oscar's head kept bobbing, and Monique's hips kept swaying, mocking her mood. Soon Liselle wanted to scream.

"I gotta go," she blurted suddenly. "I'll talk to you later, all right?"

"Girl, where you going? You just got here!" Monique exclaimed.

"I forgot—my mom, she wants me

home early tonight."

Monique chuckled. "Since when do you listen to her?"

"Since whenever, I just gotta go, okay?" Liselle snapped impatiently. Overhead, billowy gray clouds were gathering. The air felt thick and heavy and a sharp wind was beginning to blow.

Perfect, Liselle thought bitterly.

"Whatever," Monique sighed, glancing up at the sky. "Looks like it's gonna storm soon anyway. Happy Friday."

Liselle walked across the crowded parking lot, trying hard not to look at Oscar or at Kendra, who was standing with a group of seniors. Liselle pulled up her hood and turned up the music on her headphones.

Please let the test be wrong.

A raindrop slapped against her cheek. Liselle wiped it away, only to be hit again with another one. She walked quickly, trying to forget Oscar and the test and the awful, growing sense that a storm was coming.

And she was alone in the middle of it.

Chapter 3

Pregnant.

Liselle whispered the word to herself. It was Sunday evening. She had spent most of the weekend hiding in her bedroom, ignoring the phone calls from Monique. She didn't want to go to Damian's party. She didn't want to leave the house at all.

Mom had worked a double shift Saturday and the morning shift today as a waitress at Jackson's Diner. Liselle's older brother Brian had gone out with his friends, like he usually did. Liselle was glad to have the house to herself. She needed time to think. But the more she thought, the sicker she felt. It had been two days since she had taken the pregnancy test, and it still didn't seem real. What if it was true?

You should tell somebody. Kendra's advice echoed in her head.

Liselle knew the girl was right, but it seemed that as long as she didn't tell anyone, she could pretend everything was normal. The positive test result never happened. Maybe it would all just disappear somehow. But if she said the words to another person, it would be real. Everything she knew would change. The thought made her stomach tremble and her heart race. She couldn't handle it. Instead she had stayed inside her cluttered bedroom, sleeping as much as possible and staring out the window at the busy street outside. It was still raining.

"Liselle, it's almost dinnertime!" Mom yelled from the hallway. "You can't just sleep all day! Don't you have homework to do?"

Liselle groaned at the sound of Mom's voice.

"I'm not hungry!" Liselle shouted back, covering her face with a pillow. She felt dizzy and anxious. She hadn't eaten much since Friday, just a leftover piece of meatloaf and half a tuna sandwich. Each time she got hungry, she resisted the urge to eat. Her cousin

32

Shayna had complained that she was starving during most of her pregnancy.

If I'm not hungry, Liselle told herself, *then maybe I'm not pregnant either.*

"Then you can sit at the table and not eat," Mom replied. "I haven't seen you all weekend. This is my one night off and I'd like us to spend some time together."

Liselle rolled her eyes and dragged herself up from the bed and out into the small living room of their rented house. She felt shaky. A faint headache pulsed behind her tired eyes.

Mom was in the kitchen, tossing a bowl of lettuce and tomatoes. On top of the stove was a frozen pizza that Mom had warmed up in the oven. Brian was sitting on their battered couch, playing a loud video game. The thin cushions sagged beneath his weight.

"Girl, what happened to you?" he said with a smirk. The sound of gunfire and rapid flashes of light filled the room. "No offense, but you don't look so good."

"Shut up," she grumbled, flashing him an annoyed glare. She was wearing baggy sweatpants and an oversized T-shirt. She glanced at her stomach and resisted the urge to tug at the front of her shirt. "I just don't feel good."

"Are you sick?" Mom said, putting a hand on her forehead.

"I'm fine," Liselle complained, brushing her hand away, "I'm just tired."

"Well, you've been sleeping since I got home today. I haven't seen you eat a thing, either. Are you sure nothing's wrong?"

"I'm fine, Ma," Liselle insisted, slumping into a chair at their small kitchen table. She didn't like when Mom treated her like a little kid. Ever since Brian got kicked out of Bluford last year, Mom had treated her differently—as if she expec-ted Liselle to do something wrong, too.

Liselle still remembered the day Brian lost it when he found out his girl-friend, Jocelyn Harris, cheated on him.

Monique had come racing to Liselle's locker with the news.

"It was crazy, girl!" Monique had explained. *"He kept screaming how he trusted her, but she tore his heart out. I swear, he looked like he was going to hit her. And when Security tried to grab him, he punched a guard in the face. I think he broke his nose!"*

Brian never talked about it. Afterward,

Mom had to transfer him to a disciplinary program at Lincoln High School on the other side of town. She had taken a second job as a bartender to pay for Brian's bus fare and program fees.

At first, Liselle hadn't liked her mother's new schedule. But Liselle had discovered that there were benefits to Mom's long hours at work. She didn't have as much time to check Liselle's homework or make sure that Liselle was home after school. Liselle had grown used to feeling more independent. She didn't like answering her mother's questions anymore.

"Okay," Mom sighed, looking at the bubbly pizza on the stove. "I think it's done. Brian, come sit down and *please* turn off that video game." Mom rubbed her head wearily. "It sounds like a war zone in here."

Mom plopped down a thin, soggy piece of pizza in front of Liselle. "Brian, your father called. He won't be able to drive you to school tomorrow morning."

"Figures," Brian grumbled, his eyes still glued to the TV screen. He pressed hard on the controller and gunned down his opponent. The body collapsed into a pool of blood on the TV screen.

"Did Dad ask for me?" Liselle said, her face brightening.

Mom hesitated for a moment, then smiled gently. "It was a quick phone call, Liselle. We didn't have time to get into much."

Mom looked out the small window over the kitchen sink. Raindrops left long streaks against the glass, like watery fingernails trying to claw their way inside.

"He said he was gonna start helping out more since I took that second job," Mom murmured to herself. "So much for that."

"He's just *busy*, Mom," Liselle snapped. "Why you always gotta be so hard on him?"

"Well, I'm busy too, Liselle," Mom answered sternly. "A little bit of help, that's all I'm asking for. And while we're on the topic, I need you and your brother to start helping out around the house more. This place is filthy. You two are old enough to pick up after yourselves."

Liselle's parents had never been married. Dad lived nearby in a small one-bedroom apartment. Liselle didn't see him often, but whenever she did, he always brought gifts for her and her brother. Brian never spoke much to Dad. He usually gave Liselle whatever gift Dad had brought for him, like the iPod she carried to school each day.

"I don't want nothin' from that man," Brian would grumble. But Liselle loved her dad. He never grilled her about homework the way Mom did, or complained that she was watching too much television.

For Christmas, Dad had given her a small red cell phone. Liselle was thrilled but Mom had objected, arguing with Dad that Liselle was too young to have her own phone.

"Her grades are slipping and I'm not thrilled with her attitude lately, Eddie," Mom had said sternly. *"A cell phone is a privilege, and frankly, I don't think she's earned it."*

"Don't be so hard on her," Dad had replied, winking at Liselle. *"Of course she deserves it. She's my baby girl."*

Mom had reluctantly agreed after Liselle promised to improve her grades. But she knew Mom didn't like the idea. *She's just jealous because Daddy buys me gifts*, Liselle had thought bitterly. *I don't know why she's always so hard on him.*

"How's school going, baby?" Mom asked, sitting down next to her daughter.

Liselle pushed away the slice of pizza and crossed her arms. "Fine, I guess."

"Brian, please turn off that video game and come sit down," Mom said, spooning out salad onto Liselle's plate.

"In a sec," Brian answered. His eyes were glued to the TV screen. "I just gotta finish this level."

"I'm not hungry. Can I go to my room?" Liselle complained, standing up from her chair. Her eyes went blurry for a moment and her body swayed slightly. She put a hand on the table, steadying herself. She was glad Mom didn't notice. Her eyes were on Brian. A short, loud burst of gunfire blared from the TV.

"*Now*, Brian!" Mom yelled. "Liselle, sit down. We're a family, and we are going to act like it and eat dinner together!"

"It's not like you *made* dinner," Liselle grumbled. "It's frozen pizza, Ma. Who cares?"

Mom's eyes drifted to the floor and she sat back in her chair, tossing her paper napkin on the table.

"*I* care," she said.

"Yo, Liselle, what's your problem?"

Brian called from the couch. "Stop jumpin' on Mom. You know she ain't got time to be makin' no fancy dinner. Besides," he continued, looking her up and down, "it's not like you starvin'. You startin' to look kinda chunky, if you ask me."

Liselle flushed with anger and embarrassment. "Shut up, Brian. All you do is sit in front of the TV when you're here, so don't be yellin' at me!"

"That's enough!" Mom said sternly. "I know I haven't been home a lot, but we have bills to pay, and I gotta keep food on the table. You think I want to spend all my time workin'?"

Liselle glared at Brian. He shrugged his shoulders and turned off the video game.

"Now I'm counting on both of you to help me by staying out of trouble when I'm not home, and not fighting when I am. You hear me?"

"Yeah," Liselle answered weakly, avoiding Mom's weary eyes. In her mind, the blue plus sign from her pregnancy test flashed like a scene from a nightmare. It was all too much.

Back in her bedroom, Liselle curled

up into a ball. The room spun around her.

You're hungry, said a voice from deep inside her body. *You need to eat something.*

No, Liselle thought angrily.

You gotta tell somebody, the voice continued.

No, Liselle insisted, clutching her blanket and willing herself back to sleep.

By lunchtime on Monday, Liselle knew she didn't have much time left. All morning she had felt dizzy. She had trouble staying awake during class. And now, in the noisy cafeteria of Bluford High, she held onto the sides of the table, afraid to stand up.

Raindrops dripped down the windows that lined the room. Sneakers squeaked on the wet and muddy tile floor. Monique and several other girls chatted on either side of her, going on excitedly about Damian's party Saturday night.

"Girl, I don't know *why* you didn't come," Monique said, nudging Liselle.

Across the room, Oscar was sitting with his cousin Jamil and a group of friends. Liselle thought she saw Jamil look over at her, then nudge Oscar, who smiled reluctantly and turned away. Jamil laughed.

Kendra was there as well, sitting with a group of senior girls. Liselle's head throbbed and the room began to spin, slowly at first, then faster. The voices around her seemed to get louder, as if everyone was suddenly shouting. She looked in Kendra's direction. Though she wasn't sure why, she almost hoped the girl would see her and come over.

You gotta tell somebody.

"Something's wrong with me," Liselle blurted, to no one in particular.

"Huh?" said Monique.

"Something's wrong."

"Yo girl, you don't look so good," said another girl. "You sick or something?"

"Yeah," Liselle said weakly. "I mean, no. I don't know."

"Liselle!" she heard Monique exclaim, though her voice sounded far away and fuzzy. Slowly, the room began to fill with darkness, as if a heavy gray cloud of smoke was creeping in from all sides. Monique's worried face faded from sight until all Liselle could feel was the cold, wet floor against her face.

Liselle heard the squeak of Mom's rubber-soled work shoes against the floor of the nurse's office. She opened her eyes and fought back a wave of dizziness.

"What happened?" Mom said to the nurse. Her voice was tense and full of concern. "You mean, she just fainted? For no reason?"

"I'm sure there's a reason, Ms. Mason," the nurse replied. "We just don't know what it is yet. Her friends say she didn't eat much today. But that doesn't cause a healthy sixteen-year-old to pass out. Fortunately, she was only unconscious for a few seconds. And she was able to walk herself to the office. Still, I'd suggest bringing her to a doctor as soon as possible. Maybe it's nothing, but better to be safe than sorry."

"Oh don't worry," Mom replied. "We're going to the doctor right now. I don't know how I'm gonna pay for it yet, but I'll think of something."

Liselle's pulse quickened at the word *doctor*.

"I'm fine," she groaned, trying to sit up on the cold vinyl cot. "I just fell. That's all." She imagined what she must have looked like to everyone in the cafeteria. She pictured Oscar's cousin laughing at her, Kendra shaking her head, a doctor examining her stomach.

You need to tell Mom the truth. Now, insisted the voice in her ahead.

I can't! she thought desperately. Again the room seemed to spin.

"Easy, sweetheart," the nurse said. She sat next to Liselle and gently handed her a paper cup. "Here, drink some more orange juice. You'll feel better."

Liselle drank the juice in three gulps, surprised by how thirsty she was. Her stomach growled loudly and caused both women to look at her, then at each other.

"Sounds like someone's hungry," said the nurse. "How have you been feeling lately? Have you been sick?"

"No," Liselle blurted, glancing at Mom. "I mean, not really," she added weakly. "A little, maybe."

"Mrs. Wilkins, would you mind giving me a moment alone with my daughter?" Mom asked. Her light brown eyes were fixed on Liselle.

"I'm fine, Mom!" Liselle insisted once the nurse had left. "For real. I don't need to go to no doctor. Just go back to work, okay?"

"Liselle, you *fainted.* Of course we're

going to the doctor! And why haven't you been eating? What on earth is going on, baby?"

"Ma, please," Liselle pleaded, unable to hide the panic that was building inside of her, tightening like a rope around her heart. "I'm fine, I swear." Liselle knew she sounded desperate, but she couldn't help it.

Mom sat down next to her and stroked the side of Liselle's face.

"Baby, we're going to the doctor," she said firmly. "Now, I don't know what's going on, but if there's something you want to say—if you're sick, or upset— whatever it is, you need to tell me. Understand? I'm your mother. We're in this together."

For a moment, Liselle felt like a little girl again. She imagined curling up into her mother's lap and closing her eyes. For the past two days, she had tried to wish away the truth. *Maybe for the past few months*, Liselle realized with a pang of guilt. But the longer she pretended nothing was wrong, the more she tried to starve and sleep the problem away, the sicker she felt.

What else can I do? Liselle thought, looking into her mother's concerned eyes. *I gotta tell somebody.*

"It's okay," Mom promised. "Just tell me."

"I think . . ." Liselle began, but the words got stuck in her throat.

"What, baby? What is it?"

"I think I'm pregnant."

Chapter 4

An hour later, Liselle and Mom sat in a stark white room at the Brown Street Women's Health Clinic. When they had first arrived, a nurse took a urine sample and several vials of blood from Liselle. She also checked her weight and blood pressure. Then Dr. Styles, a stern-faced woman with dark skin and braids pulled back tightly, came into the room.

"Well, you're definitely pregnant," she said somberly, washing her hands at a small sink in the corner of the exam room. "Let's take a look and see how you're doing."

Dr. Styles spread cold jelly across Liselle's soft stomach and pressed a strange, microphone-shaped instrument into her abdomen. A fuzzy, gray-and-black image appeared on a computer screen next to the examination table. Mom leaned forward and looked closely; Liselle turned away, disturbed by the thought of seeing her insides projected on a TV screen for everyone to see. She felt exposed, as if someone was reading her diary out loud.

"You're about four months along," the doctor announced once the examination was done. "Everything looks fine and perfectly normal."

Mom shook her head, as if she couldn't believe what she was hearing. "Normal," she sighed. Liselle couldn't tell if she was relieved or disappointed.

"You're lucky nothing worse happened, Liselle. Your blood sugar is very low, which is not good. From now on, you *must* eat regularly. Can you tell me why you haven't been?"

Liselle shrugged. "I just wasn't hungry," she answered grumpily.

"I'll leave you with some information on how to maintain a healthy diet," the doctor said. "And I'd like you to come back on Friday at 3:30 for a follow-up visit."

Mom hadn't said much since they had left Bluford. Her arms were crossed tightly and she was biting her top lip, the way she did the day Brian was kicked out of school. Just an hour ago, sitting in the nurse's office, Liselle had felt close to Mom. But now, although her mother sat only a few feet from her, Liselle felt as if they were miles apart.

I should've kept my mouth shut, she thought.

"The pregnancy is into its second trimester," the doctor continued, looking at both of them. "Which means Liselle's options are limited. I don't know if you two have talked about what Liselle wants to do, but at this advanced stage—"

"I understand," Mom interrupted, putting up her hand as if she had heard enough.

Understand what? Liselle wondered. But the doctor kept talking, saying large, strange words that scared Liselle, even though she didn't know what they meant.

Folic acid. Ultrasound. Genetic testing. Prenatal. Fetus.

Then she handed Liselle a bottle of large purple vitamins, instructing her to take one each day, and left the room, her thick rubber shoes squeaking on the water that Liselle and Mom had tracked inside.

Liselle looked at the bottle suspiciously. "I ain't takin' these," she complained. "They're gigantic."

Mom shot her an icy glare that told Liselle she should stop talking.

As soon as they arrived home, Mom exploded.

"I can't believe this!" she hollered, throwing her bag on the couch. "Liselle, how could you let this happen? How *could* you? And how have you been hiding it all this time? I didn't even know you had a boyfriend!"

"I don't!" Liselle answered quickly, as if admitting she had a boyfriend would make things worse.

"Well, then, *who?*" Mom asked, her face a mixture of anger and concern.

"He's nobody," Liselle interrupted.

"His *name*, Liselle," Mom commanded. "What's his name?"

"Oscar, all right?" Liselle snapped. "Stop yelling at me, Mom! It's not like I did this on purpose!"

"But you still did it!" Mom replied sharply. "Liselle, we've talked about sex. We've talked about protection. I thought you were smarter than this!"

"Well, I guess I'm just stupid then! It just happened, Mom, all right? What do you want me to say?"

"Why didn't you tell me sooner?" Mom continued. "Four months along, Liselle? Why didn't you say something?"

Liselle lowered her eyes and fiddled with the drawstring on her sweatpants. "I don't know. I didn't want it to be true, I guess. I didn't want you to be mad at me."

"Well, it's too late for that!" Mom fumed, throwing her hands up in frustration.

Mom gripped Liselle by the shoulders. Their faces were only inches apart. Liselle tried to look away, but Mom held on tighter, pressing her fingernails into Liselle's skin. She smelled like diner food and perfume. Her plastic name tag hung limply from her uniform.

"Do you understand what's happening here?" Mom continued, shaking her like she was a child who tried to touch the stove. Her voice was urgent and tense. "Tell me you understand! Come summertime, you *will* have a baby. That's the reality, Liselle."

Mom continued, "I don't know what you've been thinking these past four months, but the time for pretending is over. The sooner you realize that, the sooner we can start figuring out how in the world we're gonna deal with this situation. We have a lot to work out, and not much time."

Summertime? Liselle thought. *I was gonna work at the mall with Monique this summer.*

Liselle felt as if the floor beneath her had suddenly disappeared, and she was falling, about to crash. She wished she could go back in time, to before she had taken the stupid test, to before she had ever met Oscar. But now that Mom knew the truth, there was no more pretending.

She really was pregnant. A baby really was coming. Her life was changing.

Mom released Liselle and collapsed into their worn couch.

"How could you do this, Liselle? Don't you realize what this means?"

"It can't be *that* bad, Mom," Liselle snapped, trying to sound unafraid. "I mean, Shayna had a baby. And what about you? Weren't you like, seventeen, when you had Brian?"

"Yes I was," Mom answered sharply. "And I hoped that you would learn from my mistakes."

"Oh, so me and Brian are mistakes?" Liselle snapped.

"No, that's not what I'm saying!" Mom fired back, rubbing her temples as if the conversation pained her. "Liselle, listen to me. This isn't about just you anymore. Caring for a baby is a huge responsibility. You gotta put your own needs aside and do what's best for your child. Every *day*. You don't get to take a day off or skip one night 'cause you're tired. Understand? It's not about what *you* want, it's about what the child *needs*. You ready for that?"

Liselle shrugged. The floor kept sinking. She kept falling.

"I don't know how we're gonna pay for everything," Mom continued. "I can barely afford our bills now. How in the world am I gonna afford a child?"

Mom's words made Liselle cringe. "You actin' like *you're* the one who's pregnant!" she said. "Now you know why I never told you."

Mom sighed and glanced at the clock. "I have to go back to work," she said. "Lord knows I can't get fired now. We have much more to talk about, young lady, but for the moment I want you to stay in this house until I get home tonight. And from now on, I want you coming home straight after school. Things are gonna change around here. You're gonna have to grow up real fast, Liselle. We have a lot to figure out."

"We ain't gotta figure out nothin'," Liselle grumbled, unable to stop herself. "Maybe I don't need your help."

"Baby girl," Mom said, pointing a stern finger. "You need me now more than you ever have."

Liselle stormed down the hallway, nearly slamming into her brother, who had emerged sleepily from his room.

"What's going on?" he said, rubbing his eyes. "Why's everyone yelling?"

"Leave me alone," she spat, closing her bedroom door.

Liselle could feel the blood pumping in her heart. She waited until she heard her mother leave for work. Then she searched the cluttered closet floor until she found the only bag she had, a pink duffel bag with fuzzy yellow hearts that Dad had given her years ago. It was a little girl's bag, but it would have to do. She stuffed it full with several days' worth of clothes, her favorite pajamas, and her iPod. She scanned her shelves for anything else she might need but decided to leave it all behind.

I don't need nothin' from this house, she swore.

Brian was sitting on the couch in the living room watching TV. Liselle crept into the kitchen and grabbed a handful of cereal bars from the cabinet, then headed for the door.

"Yo, where you think you're going?" Brian called from the couch.

"Out!" Liselle answered.

"No you ain't!" he snapped. "Mom said you're supposed to stay home. She's makin' me stay home just so I can watch you. What'd you do anyway?"

Liselle didn't slow down. "Tell Mom she don't gotta worry about me no more," she spat. "I don't need her help."

"Liselle!" Brian shouted. "Get back here!"

"You ain't my father," Liselle shouted. "You can't tell me what to do."

Suddenly, Brian rose from the couch and grabbed her arm. His eyes flashed with anger.

"You better watch what you say to me," he growled.

"Let go of me!" she yelled, trying to yank her arm away. She was surprised at how strong Brian's grip was.

Brian stared at her angrily.

"Please," she pleaded, lowering her eyes. "I gotta go, all right? You don't understand!"

Brian stared at her for several seconds.

"Whatever," he grumbled, letting her go as if her touch bothered him somehow. "Do what you want. I can't take you girls and all your psycho drama anyway."

"I ain't psycho," Liselle huffed. She turned away and rushed outside with her bag.

Liselle knew where she had to go, but she had to stop somewhere else first. Though she didn't want to admit it, she had to see Oscar.

It was almost 7:00 p.m. when Liselle climbed onto the crowded bus. Her heart was racing and her hands shook as she ripped the wrapper from a cereal bar. She ate it quickly, surprised at how hungry she was. Several minutes later, she got off at 51st Street and headed up the block.

A light, steady mist swarmed in the night sky. Under the yellow glow of the streetlights, the tiny raindrops looked like insects. Liselle pulled her jacket tight and stared at the white house in the middle of the block. The light was on in the living room. On the second floor, the light was on in Oscar's room, too.

Liselle pulled out her cell phone and scrolled down to Oscar's phone number.

"I'm outside," she texted. "We need to talk."

A figure soon appeared in the window and peered down at her.

"Now?" he texted back.

"It's important," she replied. Then, after a moment, "Please."

Liselle waited for what felt like several minutes. Finally, Oscar emerged from the front door of his uncle Russell's house. He crossed the street quickly and stopped a few feet from Liselle. He was wearing baggy jeans and an oversized white T-shirt. He shoved his hands in his pockets.

"What's up?" he said, his voice flat. "I can't talk long. I'm kinda in the middle of something." He glanced at the pink bag that hung from Liselle's shoulder. "What're you doing here?"

Liselle suddenly felt embarrassed by how she looked. Her jeans were wet at the bottom from the puddles she had walked through. Her stomach felt swollen and still sticky from the remnants of the ultrasound gel.

"I gotta tell you something," Liselle began.

Oscar shifted his weight from one foot to another.

He wants me to leave, she thought. *He wants me to go away.*

She wasn't really surprised. But it had been several months since she had gone near him. She had forgotten how frustrated he could make her feel. She had forgotten how much it stung.

She looked him over, trying to remember the Oscar she had met in September just across the street from where they now stood.

That night, Oscar's cousin Jamil was throwing a party. The house was crowded and loud, brimming with Bluford students. Music thumped loudly. Some kids were drinking alcohol from large plastic cups and smoking cigarettes. A cloud of gray smoke hung in the air.

Liselle walked outside to the front porch. A boy was sitting on the steps alone. Wearing baggy jeans and an oversized T-shirt, he seemed to blend into the nighttime darkness, his broad shoulders hunched over as if he was trying to make himself small. He rubbed his head as if he had a headache.

"Oh, sorry," she said, eyeing him cautiously. "I didn't know anybody was out here." She had never seen him before, and she wasn't sure if he had been drinking.

"It's cool," he answered, glancing up at her. His voice was strong, and his light-brown eyes were sharp and clear. "You can hang out." The boy stared off into the street again. "It ain't my house," he mumbled.

Liselle couldn't be sure, but she thought he sounded a bit sad. She watched him for a moment. He was tall, she thought. He had a wide face and sharp jaw line. His black hair was cut very short. Under the dim porch light, she could see the muscles moving in his long arms as he clenched and unclenched his hands.

"How come you out here all by yourself?" she asked, hoping he hadn't noticed her staring.

The boy shrugged. "Just not in the mood for all this, I guess."

"These parties can get a little crazy, that's for sure," she said shaking her head. "Last month I actually saw some kid get sick all over a girl. The boy was so drunk, he kept tryin' to talk to her, like nothin' ever happened. I ain't never seen a girl get so mad before."

"That's nasty," he chuckled. His dark skin glowed in the dim yellow porch light.

"I'm Liselle," she said, sitting down next to him.

"Oscar," he answered with a nod. "Jamil's cousin. I just moved here a couple days ago."

"So you're going to Bluford this year?"

"Yeah," he sighed. "I used to go to Lincoln, but my mom's outta work and . . ." He stopped talking and looked at Liselle, as if he was deciding what to tell her.

"Anyway," he continued. "I'm stayin' here for a while, I guess."

"That's cool," Liselle replied. She understood how hard it was to start at a new school, where nobody knew you. She had come to Bluford her freshman year from a grade school that very few of the other kids had gone to. Even though she had been at Bluford for more than two years, sometimes she still felt out of place.

"I hate school, but Bluford ain't all that bad. I mean, some of us are nice." Liselle smiled and nudged Oscar gently with her shoulder. "I ain't that terrible, right?"

Oscar let out a small chuckle. His eyes twinkled and his whole body seemed to relax a little. "Nah, you seem all right," he said, smiling at her. "So, what about you? How come you ain't in there gettin' all crazy?"

Liselle shrugged. "Maybe I'm just takin' a break," she said with a grin. "Maybe I heard there was some lonely boy sittin' out here like he's all depressed about somethin'."

Oscar laughed again gently.

"It's too crazy in there," she continued, suddenly feeling shy. "Those boys are all drunk and actin' stupid. I ain't got time for that."

Oscar looked up at her words, as if he was impressed. "I hear that," he agreed.

Suddenly, two students stumbled through the front door and bumped into Liselle.

"Yo, watch where you're goin'!" Liselle hollered.

"Sorry," the boy mumbled as he headed down the walkway with the girl.

"Man, I can't take this," Oscar blurted, standing up suddenly. "Let's get outta here."

"Where we gonna go?" Liselle asked, surprised.

"We could go up to my room," he suggested. "It's the only place I know around here. It ain't much, but at least it's quiet."

For a moment, Liselle hesitated. She wasn't sure about being alone with a boy she had just met. But there was something genuinely nice about Oscar, she thought.

Moments later, she was following him up the scuffed stairwell to his cramped bedroom. The floor was cluttered with piles of clothes and unopened cardboard boxes. He cleared a spot, and they sat together against the wall. Then they listened to music, and Oscar showed her pictures of his old friends from Lincoln High. Soon they were talking about Bluford, and she told him which teachers to avoid.

"To tell you the truth, I didn't wanna move here or go to Bluford. The only good thing about this is that I get to see my cousin Jamil. He was like an idol to me when we were growing up. At least now we finally can hang out."

"Maybe it won't be the only good thing you find out here. You never know, right?" Liselle said, surprised and a bit embarrassed about how her words sounded, especially since she was alone in a strange boy's bedroom.

Oscar smiled, and the room got quiet. Then he looked at her the way guys do just before they lean in for a kiss. Liselle's heart had raced with an electric mixture of excitement and nerves. His face crept closer until their lips touched, and she felt his warm hand wrap around her waist and touch the skin at the base of her spine. Liselle jumped, surprised at the feeling of Oscar's hand. Then she giggled and pulled away.

"I should go," she said softly. "It's late."

As they walked down the stairs, Jamil was standing with three other boys in the living room. They stopped talking at the sight of Liselle. Jamil arched an eyebrow and looked her over. He smirked and nudged the boy standing next to him. Then he looked at Oscar and nodded his head approvingly.

"Nice going, cuz," he murmured with a sly smile. "You work fast, huh?" The other boys chuckled and stared at Liselle. One of them moved his eyes across her body. Liselle knew instantly what they were thinking. She and Oscar had been upstairs for a long time.

"We were just talkin'," she snapped, trying her best to sound tough. But Jamil only chuckled. She felt ashamed in front of him, even though she had no reason to. She waited for Oscar to speak up, to say that nothing had happened or at least tell Jamil to shut up. But Oscar stayed quiet, holding the door open for Liselle but avoiding her eyes. He looked ashamed, too.

"I-I guess I'll see you at school?" she stammered, suddenly unsure of what was going on.

"Yeah," Oscar answered quickly, letting the screen door close. "Definitely."

For a moment, Liselle stood alone on the porch, listening to the boys talk inside.

"Dang, cuz! I didn't know you was up there with a girl!" said Jamil.

"Seriously, bro! You just moved here and you already workin' the ladies, huh?" said another boy. Laughter erupted and she could hear the boys slap hands, like they did on the basketball court after winning a game.

"You could do better, though," Jamil continued. "Liselle, she's all right I guess. But I know other girls at Bluford who are finer than that. No offense, bro, but she's kinda rough, if you know what I mean."

"Yeah," Oscar answered weakly, and then his voice went silent.

Walking home that night, Liselle wasn't sure how she felt. She liked Oscar. And she was pretty sure Oscar liked her. But then why had he let Jamil talk about her like that? Why hadn't he spoken up?

Maybe he was just being a guy, she told herself. Guys always talk a big game, even when it's not true.

But the more she thought about it, the more anxious she became. She wanted him to like her. She wanted to keep his attention. And she was afraid that if she didn't impress him soon, he would discover that what Jamil said was right: there were prettier girls at Bluford. Why should he care about her?

And so, after school that Monday, she returned to his house and went up the stairs to his room. And when the tense moment came and he looked at her that way again, she leaned in first. She knew what she was supposed to do next.

Mom had talked to her about condoms. So did Mrs. Serento in seventh grade health class. Liselle could remember staring at the awkward diagrams of the human body in her textbook and being quizzed on the details of how pregnancy happens and how to prevent it. And she recalled the day Monique had stolen a condom from her cousin's bedroom drawer. The girls had unwrapped it and looked at it closely. Monique joked about how it looked like an obscene balloon.

"Don't you have anything?" Liselle asked Oscar that day in his room.

"Like what?" Oscar answered, staring at her in a way that made her both happy and nervous.

"Like, you know, protection," she had continued.

"Nah," he said. "You didn't bring nothin'?"

Liselle shook her head and hesitated. "I thought you'd have it."

Oscar shrugged. "I didn't exactly know you was gonna show up here like this," he said. "Next time, all right? Don't worry."

"I don't know," Liselle whispered, looking away.

For a moment they were silent until Oscar finally sighed and sat up. "Just forget it," he said, his voice flat. "It was probably a bad idea anyway."

"No, wait," Liselle said quickly. She wanted him to stay right there with her.

In that moment, it didn't matter what Mom or Mrs. Serento had told her. All that mattered was keeping Oscar's interest.

"It's cool," she had insisted.

"You sure?" he smiled, moving close to her again.

"Yeah," Liselle nodded.

Liselle couldn't believe four months had passed since then.

Chapter 5

"I'm pregnant."

The words flew from Liselle's mouth like punches. She wanted them to hit Oscar, to knock him over as he stood there with his hands in his pockets looking nervous. He froze for an instant. His mouth opened slightly.

"What?"

"I'm pregnant."

Oscar looked around as if he was being set up. He stepped closer to her, then backed away. "F-for real?" he stammered. "Are you sure?"

"Yeah," she answered, eyeing him closely. "The doctor said I'm four months."

For a moment, she felt powerful. *Now he can't run away*, she thought bitterly.

Oscar buried his face in his hands. "I

gotta think," he murmured. "I mean, are you *sure*?"

"Yeah, I'm *sure*," she snapped. "What'd you think, I'm just makin' this up?"

"Nah," he answered quickly. "I'm just, you know, surprised."

"Me too," she grumbled, crossing her arms self-consciously.

"Are you all right? I saw you fall at lunch today."

Liselle shrugged. "I'm fine, I guess," she said, knowing the words weren't true. Oscar stared at the ground. Liselle wanted him to say something to make it all better somehow, but he was silent. The misty rain swirled around them, landing on her face in tiny droplets.

She wished she had never gone back to his house that day in September. But the truth was, she *had* gone, and they had sex. And as she walked home that afternoon, months ago, Liselle was certain that Oscar believed she was special.

But the next day, when they passed in the hallway at school, he looked away nervously and didn't say a word. It was as if he didn't know who she was.

I should've screamed at him then, she thought bitterly. *I should've made a scene and told everyone that Oscar was a dog. That's what Monique would have done.*

But instead of feeling angry, Liselle felt like a failure.

What did I do wrong?

What's wrong with me?

Why won't he look at me?

The questions left a deep, aching sadness that Liselle couldn't admit or put into words. She returned to Oscar's house after school that same day and again several days later. She was determined to show—to *prove* to him—that she was worth his attention.

Three times, she went up to his room. Each time, when no one else was around, Oscar had been nice. Each time, he promised he would remember to go the drug store to get condoms. And each time, Liselle had gone along, afraid that if she argued, he would want her to leave. But at school, Oscar continued to look past her, keeping his head down as they brushed shoulders in the hallway.

Liselle finally decided she wouldn't go back anymore. Still, she secretly waited, hoping he would miss her and call. But he never did. He never said anything at all. He just ignored her, as if nothing had ever happened.

Now, standing under the yellow streetlight in front of his house, she wanted to scream at him until he ran away in fear.

Why did you ignore me like that? What did I do wrong? Liselle swallowed hard and hung her head. *Why did I keep going back?*

Oscar glanced at her bag, his eyes fearful and confused. He looked at the front door of his uncle's house, then back at Liselle.

"So, what're you gonna do?" he asked cautiously.

"I don't know," she shrugged. "I'm four months along. The doctor said I gotta keep it. My mom, she got really mad, so I left."

Oscar glanced at her bag again.

"I got a place to stay, though," she added quickly, with a touch of anger.

Oscar sighed heavily, his thick shoulders sagging like something very heavy was sitting on them. "I can't believe this," he murmured to himself. "What am I gonna do now?"

The rain began to pick up. Oscar stared at the sidewalk, the wet, cracked pavement like a watery spider web beneath his feet. Liselle waited for him to say something, to tell her he wasn't angry with her, that he was sorry for ignoring her all this time, that everything would be okay. But the words didn't come.

"I should go," he finally sighed, "My cousin, he's waitin' for me."

Liselle suddenly felt exhausted. She hoisted the bag on her shoulder and turned to leave. "I gotta go, too," she said quickly, trying her best to sound strong. "Look, I'm not askin' you for nothin'. I just thought you should know. I'll see you around, I guess."

Liselle turned and headed to the bus stop on the corner, the bag thumping against her back.

"Hold up!" Oscar called, catching up to her. "Liselle, wait." Oscar stepped in front of her, blocking her path. "Look, I'm just really surprised. I wasn't expecting this. I gotta think." Oscar rubbed his head and breathed in deeply, staring at the wet pavement as if he was figuring out what to say. Then he looked up at Liselle. "I'll call you tomorrow or something, all right?"

"I guess," she shrugged. "I mean, that'd be cool."

"I ain't mad or nothin'. I'm just, you

know, surprised."

"You ain't the only one," she sighed.

"C'mon," he said, taking her bag. "I'll wait with you till the bus comes."

The air was wet and heavy, but suddenly Liselle felt a touch of warmth deep inside her. She wasn't sure she could trust Oscar. She couldn't forget how he had ignored her all these months. But it also felt good to have him carry her bag. It felt good to think that maybe now he would talk to her again.

"Guess I'll talk to you tomorrow?" Liselle said as she climbed aboard the bus.

"Yeah," Oscar answered. "Definitely."

Oscar's shadowy outline grew smaller and smaller in the bus window. Liselle leaned back and closed her eyes. *He's gonna call me*, she thought with a smile. *He's got to call me. From now on, me and Oscar are connected. Now I'll be important to him.*

Fifteen minutes later, the bus hissed to a stop in front of a narrow beige apartment building. Liselle bounced down the steps, suddenly feeling very awake and excited. *Everything's gonna be all right*, she told herself as she pressed the button for "Mason" in apartment 3C.

"Hello?" a familiar voice crackled through the speaker.

"Daddy!" Liselle squealed. "It's me! Let me in!"

"Liselle?" her father replied, sounding surprised. "Is that you?"

"Yeah! Lemme in!" she replied with a smile. "I gotta tell you something."

The metal door buzzed and then clicked. Liselle pushed it open and bounded up the three flights of stairs. Her father was waiting at the door to his apartment, a look of confusion on his face. He was wearing a wrinkled white T-shirt and striped pajama bottoms. In the background, a basketball game played on his small TV.

"What's going on?" he asked. "It's almost 9:00 p.m.!"

Liselle hugged him tightly. "Me and Mom had a fight. I moved out."

"Moved out?" Dad chuckled. "What're you talking about? Where's your mother?"

Liselle plopped her bag on the living room floor. She had been to Dad's apartment only a handful of times. Usually he would come to their house, or he would meet her somewhere public like a restaurant or the mall. Liselle was surprised at how cramped and messy it was. There was a faint smell of dirty laundry and old food. A jacket was thrown carelessly over the back of the TV. Several empty soda cans and a half-eaten frozen dinner sat on Dad's small coffee table. A dirty shirt hung from the arm of the couch.

"She got mad at me," she answered with a shrug. "So I left. You know how she is."

Dad laughed again and shook his head. "Left? Liselle, you can't just *leave*. You're sixteen years old. Where are you gonna go?"

"I thought maybe I could live here," she answered, trying her best to sound cheerful.

"*Here?*" Dad stepped back and rubbed his forehead. "Liselle," he said, shaking his head, his words slow and deliberate, "it's great to see you, but what made you think you could live here?"

Liselle stared up at her father. "I dunno," she answered, her eyes dropping to the stained carpet beneath Dad's feet. "I just thought maybe it would be cool."

Dad shook his head. "Let's just call your mother and find out what's going on," he said, grabbing the phone off the kitchen wall. "Whatever you two were fighting about, I'm sure it's not that bad."

Liselle didn't like the way he was acting. He almost seemed annoyed at her being there, as if she was intruding on him somehow. And she didn't want him to call her mother. Mom would come over and try to pick her up. Liselle was sure of it. She was determined not to go back home. She had no choice but to tell Dad the truth. Maybe then he would let her stay with him. She took a deep breath and forced the words from her lips.

"I'm pregnant," she mumbled.

Dad jerked as if he had been hit. "What did you say?"

"I'm pregnant," Liselle repeated. "Mom started yelling, and I couldn't stand it. I thought maybe it would be cool, you know, if I could live with you instead."

"Is this some kind of joke, Liselle?"

"I'd only stay here for a little while. Just until I figure things out," Liselle explained. "You're always sayin' how you wish you could see me more. Well, maybe now you can," Liselle said, remembering how he had said the words so many times before. "I could even help you clean this place up. And maybe I could learn to cook and stuff. It won't be bad. I promise, Dad. Please?"

He stared at her for a second as if she was broken. "*Pregnant*?" he repeated.

She nodded, bothered by the look in his eyes.

For a few moments, he was silent. "I-I don't know what you want me to do here, baby," he stammered. "I really think we should call your mother."

"No!" Liselle cried. "Dad, please! I don't wanna go back there! I wanna stay here." Liselle hated the way she sounded, her voice screeching slightly like a little girl's.

Dad sighed and sat down next to her on the couch. He seemed uncomfortable. His brow was creased, as if he could barely hold back the thoughts in his head. "Liselle, I don't know what's going on here, but I think you need to get a good night's rest."

"What?" Liselle asked. *Didn't he hear me?* she wondered.

"It's late," he continued. "And you're upset. Get some sleep, and tomorrow morning we can figure this out, all right? I'll set you up on the couch here."

Dad walked into his bedroom and emerged moments later with a towel, some wrinkled sheets and a limp pillow.

"Here you go," he said, his voice forced and tense. "There's food in the fridge if you're hungry." She noticed that he avoided looking at her as he spoke.

Why was he acting this way? What was he thinking? she wondered.

"Are you mad at me?" she asked when she couldn't stand it anymore.

"Of course not," Dad insisted. "I just . . . think we both need to get some rest, okay? We'll talk about this tomorrow." Dad gave her a quick kiss on the forehead and retreated to his room. "G'night, baby," he murmured and shut the door.

Liselle rummaged through Dad's refrigerator. There wasn't much, just some milk and a carton of leftover Chinese food. She made herself a bowl of cereal. Then she took a shower and changed into her pajamas.

Dad's just surprised, that's all, she told herself. *In the morning, he'll be glad I'm here.*

Liselle turned off the light and TV and sank down into Dad's lumpy couch. She imagined Oscar calling her tomorrow.

Maybe he would even come with her to the doctor on Friday.

"It'll be okay," Liselle whispered to herself, hoping she was right.

Staring at the ceiling of the dark apartment, Liselle could hear the vibration of the neighbor's TV through the living room wall. In the hallway, two women were speaking Spanish. She noticed another sound too—Dad's voice from behind his bedroom door. His light was still on. His voice, though soft, sounded tense.

I thought he was going to sleep, Liselle thought. She sat up and crept over to the door, but she couldn't make out what he was saying. Then she spotted the phone on the kitchen wall. She gently lifted the receiver and held it up to her ear.

"Gloria, you *have* to come get her!" Dad fumed. "This is ridiculous! How could you let this happen?"

Liselle cringed, nearly dropping the phone. She couldn't believe he was talking this way about her to Mom.

"Eddie," Mom replied, her voice calm but stern, "Don't you dare suggest this is my fault. She's your daughter, too, remember? Frankly, I think she could use some fatherly advice right now. Maybe staying with you for a while would be good for her."

"Don't you try to make this my problem," Dad shot back. "You know she can't live here. She lives with you! That's the way it's always been! And especially *now!* I mean, *Gloria*," Dad continued. He sounded as if he was talking to a child. "What am I gonna do with her and a baby?"

"She's not having the baby for five months. Calm down," Mom said.

Dad took a deep strained breath. "You know who this baby's father is?" he asked. "He even gonna help her?"

"I don't know anything, Eddie. I just learned this today."

Dad cursed under his breath. "How's Liselle gonna raise a child? Huh?" he asked. "Maybe she oughta think about adoption or something. Seriously, you know she isn't ready for a baby."

"Neither were we," Mom snapped.

"Don't go there, Gloria," Dad grumbled. "That's different and you know it."

Liselle leaned her head against the wall. The room seemed to spin in the darkness. She still couldn't believe how Dad sounded.

"Look," Mom sighed. "I don't wanna go through this now. Just let her stay with you tonight. I'll come get her in the morning before school. And please *try* to talk to her. She's always looked up to you. She'll listen to you. Tell her she should come home. Tell her I'm sorry."

Liselle couldn't take it. She hung up the phone carefully and slumped back to the couch. She buried her face in her hands, her eyes burning.

He doesn't want me here, she thought. *He wants me to go away.* Part of her felt foolish for thinking he would respond differently. Another part felt ashamed, the way she did when Oscar ignored her at school.

Dad kept talking for several more minutes. Then the apartment grew quiet. She could see the shadows of his feet pacing back and forth in the light under his bedroom door. A few times, she was sure he was about to come out and talk to her. But the door never opened. Eventually, Dad's light went out.

Liselle considered packing up her things and leaving right then, but she was too exhausted to head back out in the rain. Besides, she didn't know where else to go. She closed her eyes and fell into a fitful sleep, waking up just before sunrise. Then she changed her clothes, packed her bag and wrote a short note on the back of a receipt she found crumpled on the kitchen counter.

Sorry I bothered you, she wrote. *Don't be mad. Tell Mom I'm fine.*

Liselle headed out into the wet streets, away from Bluford High. She waited until 9:00 a.m. before heading to the only place—the last place—she could think of going: her cousin Shayna's house.

Chapter 6

"Girl, I'm so excited!"

Shayna Gibbs jumped up and down in the middle of her living room floor. She clapped her hands wildly and danced in a circle, then hugged Liselle with such force that Liselle actually laughed out loud.

"This is gonna be so cool! Now you'll have a baby just like me!"

Liselle stared at her cousin with surprise. "Yeah," she answered slowly. "I guess so."

"When are you due? Have you picked out any names?"

"I haven't really thought about that kinda stuff yet," Liselle answered. "I just found out yesterday . . ."

"This is gonna be great!" Shayna interrupted with a bright smile. She was talking very quickly. "I hope you have a girl. I had so much fun dressing up Ruby when she was a baby. She looked just like a little doll. Ooh! I could give you some of her clothes! I think Mom saved them all!"

Shayna was almost two years older than Liselle. She was tall with light, almost yellow eyes and high cheekbones that seemed to jut out proudly from her face. Liselle had always looked up to Shayna. When they were young, Shayna would often sleep over her house when her mother, Aunt Zoe, was working late. Shayna was outgoing and confident in a way that Liselle admired. When Liselle was a freshman at Bluford, Shayna was a junior. She had introduced Liselle to her friends and had even let her sit with them at lunch.

Shayna dropped out of school once her daughter Ruby was born. Liselle visited a few times. But the baby cried a lot, and Shayna seemed tired and easily annoyed. Aunt Zoe was always rushing around the house, picking up toys from the floor or feeding the baby or changing her diaper. Once, Aunt Zoe had stopped Liselle at the door and told her that Shayna wasn't feeling well. Liselle could see her sitting at the kitchen table. She looked as if she had been crying.

After a while, Liselle stopped going over there. It wasn't much fun. Not like it used to be.

Is that how it's gonna be for me? Liselle wondered.

"Sorry I haven't been around lately. I've just been real busy with school and all," Liselle lied. She looked around the small apartment. The floor was littered with plastic baby toys. An empty bottle sat on the coffee table, half-filled with a white liquid. Liselle's stomach tightened. She couldn't admit it, but she didn't want to see the baby.

"Where's Ruby?" she asked, trying to hide her thoughts.

"My mom took her to the grocery store. They should be back pretty soon. You tell your mom you're pregnant yet?"

"Yeah," Liselle sighed. "She got all mad and crazy about it. Like the end of the world was comin'."

"Girl, don't listen to her," Shayna scoffed. "It ain't that bad. The first couple of months were kinda rough, but now . . ." She sat on the couch and kicked her feet up on the glass coffee table, knocking the bottle over. "It's all good. I still go out with my friends on the weekend, and Mom helps me during the week. It's not that bad."

Liselle studied her cousin. She was wearing tight-fitting jeans and a red T-shirt with the words "Super Star!" streaking across the front in silver glitter. Liselle remembered Shayna wearing the same shirt before she got pregnant last year. Her soft belly spilled out over the top of her jeans. Liselle looked away, slightly embarrassed.

"It can't be easy, though. Taking care of a baby," she said.

Shayna shrugged and grabbed a bag of potato chips from the table. "Nah," she said, crunching a chip loudly. "Not if you got help. My mom, she *loves* Ruby. She can't get enough of her. Your mom'll be the same way. You'll see. My mom, she was real mad too, but she got over it . . ." Shayna bit into another chip. "Now she takes that baby *everywhere*. I ain't gotta do nothin' most of the time."

Liselle couldn't believe what she was hearing. *Not that bad?* she thought. That's not what Mom or Dad said. Maybe they were wrong.

Liselle sat down in a large chair and felt her body relax into the soft cushions.

Shayna crunched another potato chip and grabbed the remote control, flipping on a music video channel.

I knew Mom was overreacting. Dad too, Liselle thought angrily. *Shayna knows how it is. She knows better than anyone else, maybe. And at least she's excited for me.*

"There's something else I gotta tell you," Liselle said slowly. "I kinda need a place to stay for a while. My mom, well, we got in a fight. And Dad . . ." Liselle paused and looked at her cousin, who was staring at the TV. She didn't want Shayna to know the truth. *He didn't want me. And now I got nowhere to go.*

Liselle kept her voice steady and casual. "Anyway," she continued, fiddling with the pink fuzzy handle on her damp bag. "Think I could crash here? Just for a little while, till I figure things out? I know it's a surprise and all, but—"

"It's cool with me, girl," Shayna said, plunging her hand into the potato chip bag again. "But my mom . . . she won't like it. We ain't got much room as it is."

"Oh, right," Liselle replied quickly. "I figured. I just thought I'd ask."

On the TV, a muscular guy in a tight white T-shirt sang to the camera. He clutched a rose and pounded his heart with a clenched fist. He seemed to look directly at Liselle as he sang.

> *Girl, you know you're the only one*
> *   for me*
> *Why can't you see*
> *How lost I am without you?*

Liselle looked away, her eyes burning. She turned on her cell phone and checked her texts and voicemail, hoping maybe Oscar had called, though it was still early. There were three messages, all from Mom.

I can't go back to Mom's. I won't! Liselle thought to herself. She deleted the messages without listening.

Shayna stared at the TV, her eyes barely blinking.

She probably wants me to leave too, just like Dad, Liselle thought. *What am I gonna do?*

Reluctantly, Liselle stood up with her backpack. "Guess I should get going," she mumbled. "I just wanted to say hi and tell you the news and all."

"Girl, don't leave! You just got here!" Shayna protested.

"It's like you said, Shayna. Your momma ain't gonna let me stay here."

Suddenly, a mischievous grin spread across Shayna's face. "I got it!" she exclaimed. "Oh my God, Liselle, I got it!" Shayna jumped up from the couch, scattering crumbs across the cluttered floor. "Why don't *we* move in together? We could get an apartment!" Shayna clapped her hands together as if she had just won the sweepstakes. The words flew out of her mouth like confetti.

Liselle was stunned. "For real?" she replied slowly.

Shayna's eyes were wide with excitement. "I'm serious, girl! We could take turns watching the babies! That way we'd always have a babysitter! This could be great! Me and you, girl, just like when we were kids. Remember how much fun we used to have camping out in your living room? Staying up late to watch those scary movies that came on after midnight?"

Liselle grinned at the memory. "We'd hide under the blanket and pretend we were asleep when Mom came out to check on us."

"Man, I miss those nights," Shayna laughed.

Liselle closed her eyes. She could almost feel the warmth of Mom's thick knitted blanket pulled over her head like a cocoon, the toasty blue glow of the TV filling the room. Her living room felt like the entire world to her back then: safe, warm, simple. It seemed so long ago. She wished she could turn back the clock.

"I miss 'em too," she whispered.

Shayna bounced across the room and put her arm around Liselle. "So, whatcha think, girl? Wanna be my roommate?"

"Really?" Liselle whispered, her voice shaking slightly. "You really wanna live with me?"

"You said yourself you ain't got nowhere to go," Shayna continued. "And I'm sick of livin' here anyway. Mom's always on my case about something."

"I know what you mean," Liselle chuckled. Her mind was racing. Could they really get an apartment together? Could this be the answer she had been looking for?

Living with Shayna almost seemed too good to be true—to be with someone who wouldn't be on her case all the time and who didn't treat her like a kid. But most of all, Shayna knew what it was like to have a baby. Liselle was sure she could teach her how to take care of her baby. Suddenly, becoming a mom didn't seem so scary. *If Shayna can do it,* thought Liselle, *so can I.*

"But how we gonna pay for everything?" Liselle asked, trying not to sound too excited.

Shayna waved her hands as if she was swatting away the question. "We'll figure something out. C'mon, say yes, Liselle! This could be so much fun!"

A strong gust of wind rushed into the room as the front door swung open. Aunt Zoe walked in with two bags of groceries hanging from her arm and a little girl clinging to her neck. Water dripped from her see-through plastic rain hat. She was slightly out of breath.

"Mom!" Shayna exclaimed. "Liselle's here! She's gonna have a baby too! We're gonna get an apartment together!"

Aunt Zoe looked at her daughter wearily. "Shayna, take the baby please. I need to get the groceries inside before the rain starts up again."

Shayna picked up Ruby and handed her to Liselle. The little girl was wearing a bright red coat and white tights, with shiny black shoes. She had large brown eyes, and her hair was neatly arranged into two pigtails.

The little girl stared at Liselle, her eyes slightly fearful. A frown spread across her small mouth. She began to squirm and kick her legs into Liselle's stomach. Then she let out a small cry. Liselle wondered what to do.

Aunt Zoe leaned over and took Ruby into her arms. "Hello, Liselle," she said with a weary smile. She looked much older than Liselle remembered. There were dark circles under her eyes, and deep wrinkles around her tight, serious mouth. "Shouldn't you be in school?"

"Didn't you hear me, Ma?" Shayna interrupted. "She's pregnant. She ain't gotta go to school anymore. C'mon, girl. Let's get some pizza."

"Wait," Liselle said softly as Shayna pulled her toward the front door. "Shouldn't we help your mom with the groceries?" she asked her cousin, but Shayna was already outside.

Liselle stopped at the doorway, unsure what to do. Ruby sniffled softly and buried her head into Aunt Zoe's neck. Shayna bounded down the walkway the way she did years earlier, long before she was a parent. Though she wasn't sure why, Liselle suddenly felt uneasy. She wished Shayna hadn't blurted out the news of her pregnancy like that. And what did Aunt Zoe think of all this? Would she call Mom? Would she let her stay for a little while until they found another place to live?

Everything seemed to be going fast—maybe too fast—since she had arrived at Shayna's house. Liselle felt dizzy from it all. She looked at her aunt, wondering what she should do.

"Go on," Aunt Zoe said, patting Ruby's back. "It's okay," she added, turning away with Shayna's baby. "I'll be here when you get back."

Liselle followed her cousin out into the busy streets and tried to ignore the growing feeling that things with Shayna weren't right.

Chapter 7

On Wednesday afternoon, Liselle walked up the steps to Mom's house and gently put her key in the door. Mom worked late on Wednesdays, and Brian usually stayed out with his friends until after dinnertime. Liselle needed some fresh clothes and her cell phone charger. The battery was dying, and she was afraid to miss Oscar's call.

Maybe tonight he'll call me, she thought. *Maybe he just needed time to think.*

In her bedroom, Liselle found a pile of clean laundry folded on her bed. Her comforter was pulled up neatly under her pillows, and the room smelled of dryer sheets and Mom's perfume. Liselle lay down on her soft bed and buried her face in her pillows, breathing in the clean, familiar scent. She missed her bed. And though she hated to admit it, she missed her house too.

Sleeping at Shayna's hadn't been easy. Aunt Zoe had insisted Liselle sleep on the living room sofa.

"It's the most comfortable place we got," she said.

But Shayna wanted to stay up late watching TV. Liselle couldn't sleep with the noise, so she moved to Shayna's room. The musty air mattress barely fit on the floor. Outside, sirens wailed and lights flashed through the dark room several times. When Shayna finally came to bed, she accidentally kicked Liselle's shoulder. It was 3:15 a.m. Not long after, the baby was awake and fussing. Aunt Zoe stomped in to get her at 5:30. Liselle felt as if she had been up all night.

It'll be better once we have our own place, Liselle told herself. *Then I'll have my own room. It'll be just like home.*

Home.

Her old bedroom was quiet and peaceful. Ruby wasn't there whining. The TV wasn't blaring. Aunt Zoe wasn't struggling to take care of everything. It had been two days since Liselle had felt this relaxed. She yawned and curled up on her bed, her eyes suddenly feeling heavy.

Maybe I'll just rest for a few minutes, she thought, as her mind slowly began to drift . . .

Dad was kneeling at the end of a long dark hallway, his arms open wide. "I miss you!" he exclaimed with a smile. "Come here, baby girl!"

"Daddy!" Liselle yelled, running down the hallway toward him.

But as soon as he saw her, Dad's face changed into an angry grimace. He grabbed her hard by her shoulders and began to shake her.

"What did you do?" he growled. "What's wrong with you? You've always been a burden. I never wanted you. Hear me? I don't want you."

He pushed her aside and stormed down the long, dark corridor.

"Daddy!" Liselle pleaded. She followed him into the darkness and emerged onto a familiar porch. She grabbed his shoulder. "Please don't leave me," she begged.

He turned, but when he faced her, he was no longer her father. Oscar stared back at her with the same angry expression.

"You heard me, girl," he hissed, pushing her away. " I don't want you."

"No!" she screamed.

"Liselle! Wake up!"

Liselle bolted upright, her heart pounding in her chest. She shoved away the hand from her shoulder. For a moment she didn't know where she was or who was next to her. But then she saw her brother staring down at her. It was dark outside. She must have been asleep for several hours.

"You okay? You were yelling."

"Yeah," Liselle murmured, trying to shake away the dream. "What're you doing here?"

"What're *you* doing here?" Brian answered. "I've been home for, like, an hour. I didn't even know you were in here till you started hollering. You sure you're okay?"

"I'm fine," she grumbled, shoving the laundry and her cell phone charger into her pink bag. "I just needed a couple things, that's all."

Brian's face was serious. "Look Liselle, why don't you just stay here?

Mom'll be home in a little while. She's real worried about you. She told me you're pregnant."

"You ain't gotta worry about me, Brian," Liselle snapped. "I'm fine. Me and Shayna, we're getting an apartment. I'm gonna be on my own." Liselle watched her brother carefully. She felt proud to tell him she was moving out. She wanted him to be jealous.

"Shayna?" Brian replied with surprise. "Why would you wanna live with *Shayna?"*

"Because," Liselle answered sharply. "She wants to live with me. We're gonna help each other out."

"No offense, but she ain't the most responsible girl in the world. You really wanna live with *her?* Besides, you're only sixteen. How you gonna pay for an apartment? And with a baby on top of it?"

Liselle wondered the same thing, though she wouldn't admit it to Brian. She had tried to talk to Shayna about her fears. Shouldn't they be looking for jobs and a place to live? Each time she brought it up, Shayna got annoyed. *"Girl, stop stressin',"* she would say, turning up the volume on the TV. *"We got plenty of time."*

"You're just jealous 'cause you gotta stay here with Mom," Liselle snapped, hoping to change the subject.

"Look Liselle," Brian began, sitting on the bed next to her. "I know we don't always get along, but can we be real for a second? You're gonna have a baby. You gotta start thinkin' about what's best for the kid."

"*I am*," she insisted.

"What about the father? He's gonna help you out, right?"

Liselle shrugged. "I think so," she said. "Yeah. He's gonna call me today."

"He better do more than *call* you," Brian replied, his voice suddenly angry. "He's about to be a father. Kids *need* a father. It ain't right the way guys bail on their kids around here. It makes me sick."

Liselle had never heard her brother sound so serious before. His eyes flashed with a cold hostility. "Yo, if you need me to talk to this guy for you, just tell me, Liselle. I'll teach that boy a lesson."

"I don't need you to do anything for me, Brian," Liselle said. "Promise me you're gonna stay out of this."

Brian nodded and stared out the dark window, his hands clenched into tight fists. Liselle liked that he was being protective. But part of her was frightened of the anger in his eyes. She knew about his temper—the same anger that got him kicked out of Bluford.

"I saw Dad," she admitted quickly, trying to change the subject. "I went to his place the night I left. He told Mom to come get me. He didn't want me there."

Brian shook his head, a look of disgust on his face. "That man," he grumbled. "I could've told you he'd do that. No offense, girl, but you've always had a crazy story in your head about Dad. Like he's Santa Claus or something. Yeah, he's like Santa all right—only showin' up once a year with presents, like we're supposed to be all happy 'cause he bought us stuff. That ain't a father, if you ask me. A real father spends time with his kids. A real father would help Mom out."

"I know," Liselle said weakly. "I guess I just thought . . . I dunno, I guess I thought I could change his mind. Like I could *make* him want me."

Brian looked at her thoughtfully. "You can't make nobody be nothin' they ain't," he said. "People are who they are, Liselle. If they act like fools, you should believe 'em, not try to change 'em or pretend they're something else."

Liselle listened carefully to her brother's words. She thought about Oscar. Up until now, he hadn't given her much reason to believe he would stand by her side. Did that mean she should just give up on him?

"People can change sometimes," she said.

"Maybe," Brian replied. "But you can't make 'em. They gotta do that on their own."

Liselle finished packing her bag. "I gotta go," she said reluctantly. "Don't tell Mom I was here, okay?"

Brian shrugged. "Sorry I grabbed your arm the other night. I just got mad, you know?"

"Yeah," Liselle replied. Outside, it was starting to rain again. Liselle sighed wearily, wishing she didn't have to make the long trip back to Shayna's.

Brian handed her a crumpled twenty-dollar bill. "Just take it. Be safe. I'm that baby's uncle. Remember that," he said as she walked down the stairs into the rain.

On Thursday night, Aunt Zoe announced she was going out. She emerged from her bedroom dressed in a shiny blue skirt and matching top. Her hair was pressed smooth and her lips shined with pale red lipstick. Her pointy black shoes clicked on the wood floors.

"Girls, I'm going to dinner," she said.

Liselle was surprised at how pretty she looked. Usually she had a burp cloth draped over her shoulder, or a stained apron tied around her waist. Her eyes seemed to sparkle with energy.

"You look nice," Liselle said with a smile.

"Thank you," she replied proudly. She glanced at Shayna, who was rummaging through the refrigerator. "It's been quite a while since I've gone out. I'm having dinner with my friends from church. We might even go to the movies. You girls will have to put Ruby to bed tonight."

Aunt Zoe looked at Shayna and sighed. "But maybe I should cancel. Ruby's been fussy today."

"She's fine, Ma," Shayna said quickly. "Don't worry. We got it. Right, Liselle?"

"There's a bottle in the fridge. Warm it up and feed her before bedtime. I'll have my cell phone on all night if you need me. The number's on the fridge."

"Have fun!" Shayna exclaimed, her voice oddly cheerful. Shayna flashed a quick grin at Liselle, as if they were sharing a secret, though Liselle didn't know what it was.

"Yeah, have fun," Liselle replied, looking at the baby nervously. Ruby was sitting on the floor, a rattle clutched in her small hand. Liselle had never taken care of a young child before—or any child, for that matter. For the past few days, she had actually avoided Ruby. She tried to pay attention to all that Aunt Zoe did to care for her, but in truth, it seemed overwhelming. Boring, even. Bottles. Diapers. Food. Bathing. She was amazed at how much her aunt did. Sometimes it seemed as if she didn't stop moving all day.

Shayna knows what to do, Liselle assured herself. *It's only for a few hours. Besides, maybe me and Shayna can talk about where we're gonna live.*

But as soon as her mother left, Shayna jumped up from the couch and disappeared into her room. She returned a short time later wearing a snug skirt, black boots and a shiny black top that plunged low on her chest. She put a hand on her hip and arched her back the way models do at the end of a fashion runway.

"How do I look?" she asked Liselle with a mischievous grin.

"Good, I guess," Liselle replied uncertainly. "Why you all dressed up?"

"You gotta cover for me, girl. I'm going out."

"Going out?" Liselle repeated nervously. "Whatcha mean, Shayna?" She watched as her cousin slipped on her puffy red coat and fixed her lipstick in the mirror. "But we gotta watch the baby."

"I won't be that long," Shayna replied, flashing her a smile. "Besides, you need the practice, right? You gonna have your own baby soon enough."

Is she kidding? Liselle wondered.

Shayna grabbed her cell phone from the coffee table and kissed Ruby on the head. Ruby smiled and tried to grab the zipper on her mother's coat. "Bye, baby girl," Shayna said.

"Shayna, you can't just leave," Liselle repeated, her voice rising in fear. "I can't take care of her by myself. She don't even know me! I think I make her nervous."

"Don't be stupid," Shayna answered. She sounded slightly annoyed. "Just be cool, a'ight? It ain't that complicated. Just give her a bottle and put her to bed. I'll be back before you know it."

"Shayna, wait!" Liselle pleaded, following her to the door. "I got a bad feeling about this. Seriously, you should just stay here. I thought we could look for apartments. We barely talked about how we're gonna get our own place. If you wanna see your friends, maybe me and your mom could watch Ruby Friday night or something."

Shayna chuckled bitterly. "Look, Liselle, just do me this favor. You don't understand."

"Understand what?"

"What it's like for me," she confessed. For a moment, Shayna looked sad. Her forehead wrinkled, and she shook her head, as if she was trying to shake away a thought. "I wanna go out, Liselle, all right? You owe me, anyway. I *am* letting you stay at my house, right?"

"Yeah," Liselle answered. She didn't like the way her cousin was talking to her. "I guess."

"I'll see you later. Just be cool, all right?" Shayna grabbed her jacket and headed down the hallway.

Liselle turned to face Ruby, who was

still sitting on the floor. She looked up at Liselle, her brown eyes wide and slightly nervous. "It's okay," Liselle said, forcing herself to smile. "We'll be all right."

Ruby rubbed her eyes. A trickle of mucus dripped from her tiny nose.

Liselle sat on the floor and put Ruby on her lap. *Maybe Shayna's right*, she thought, trying to calm herself. *I do need the practice, I guess.*

It was 6:00 p.m.

At 7:33 p.m., Ruby began to cry. It started softly, with a sniffle and her small mouth curling down into a frown. She was sitting on the floor, holding a stuffed puppy. She rubbed her eyes and let out a small cough.

Maybe she's tired. I should feed her, Liselle thought. She took the bottle from the fridge and ran it under warm water the way Aunt Zoe did. Ruby crawled after her, bumping her head on the refrigerator. She let out a cry that morphed into a steady loud sob.

"It's okay!" Liselle exclaimed, dropping the bottle in the sink. She scooped up Ruby. Tears streamed from Ruby's eyes. Liselle grabbed the bottle, which was still cold, and sat on the couch. She tried to get Ruby to eat, but the child squirmed away, arching her back in frustration. She looked at Liselle and let out a loud squeal.

Liselle cringed. *What's wrong?* she thought. She tried to remember what she had seen Aunt Zoe do when Ruby would cry. Liselle pressed Ruby close to her and walked around the room, bouncing her gently. She put her in her crib and whispered *hush.* She tried to give her the bottle again. But no matter what she did, Ruby kept crying. Sweat dripped down Liselle's forehead. Her head ached from the noise. Ruby clung to her shirt, her wet eyes pleading with Liselle. She was sweating, too.

"What's wrong with you!?" she imagined Ruby screaming. *"Why won't you help me?!"*

"How's Liselle gonna raise a child?" Dad's voice shouted in her head. *"You know she isn't ready for no baby!"*

Dad's words burned in her chest. In that moment, looking down at Ruby, Liselle knew they were true. More than ever, she felt lost. Panicky. Her heart began to pound. The room began to spin. Ruby's cries grew steadily louder.

"I don't know what to do!" Liselle yelled in the empty apartment. She grabbed her cell phone and called Shayna, but her voicemail answered after only one ring. Liselle left Shayna a frantic message. Ruby began to wail.

"Oh please, stop crying!" Liselle pleaded. "I don't know what to do!"

Tears sprang to Liselle's eyes. "I'm sorry!" she sobbed, hugging Ruby close to her chest. "I don't know how to take care of you." It was almost 8:30. Ruby had been crying for an hour.

"Baby girl, you need me more now than you ever have." Mom's words echoed in her head.

Is this what Mom meant? Is this what it'll be like? Liselle wondered.

She raced to the kitchen and dialed the phone number Aunt Zoe had left on the fridge.

Aunt Zoe answered immediately.

"Ruby won't stop crying!" Liselle blurted into the phone. "I've tried everything!"

"Liselle? What's wrong?!" Aunt Zoe said, her voice tense.

"I don't know! She just won't stop!" she cried.

"Where's Shayna?"

"Please, Aunt Zoe. I don't know what to do!"

Chapter 8

Ten minutes later, Aunt Zoe burst through the front door and gathered Ruby into her arms.

"What happened?" she asked, quickly scanning the apartment. Her eyes were sharp and focused. "Where's Shayna?"

Liselle was exhausted. She collapsed on the couch, covering her face with her hands. She was furious with her cousin for leaving her alone with Ruby. *Shayna lied to me,* Liselle thought angrily. *She told me that being a mom was easy. But it's only easy for her because Aunt Zoe does everything.* She had always looked up to Shayna, but suddenly she wondered if she knew her cousin at all.

"Shayna left," Liselle admitted. "She went out with her friends. I told her not to go."

Aunt Zoe shook her head angrily. "I'll deal with her later," she said in a sharp voice. Then she grabbed a small plastic thermometer from the kitchen and gently laid Ruby on the floor. "Get up, Liselle!" she insisted. "You need to learn how to do this."

Liselle watched as Aunt Zoe placed the thermometer under Ruby's arm. Moments later, it beeped and flashed "100.5" in large digital numbers.

"She has a fever, see? It's not too high. We'll give her some medicine. That should make her feel better. Now watch me . . ."

Aunt Zoe wiped Ruby's face with a cool washcloth. Then she gently squeezed a dropper-dose of purple liquid into Ruby's mouth. She spoke to Ruby in a soft, loving voice, reassuring her that everything was okay, that Grandma was here. After a while, Ruby quieted down. Aunt Zoe sat next to Liselle and handed her the sleepy child. Ruby curled up against her. Her eyes sagged sleepily.

"Is she okay?" Liselle asked, staring down at Ruby's contented round face.

"She'll be fine," Aunt Zoe sighed. "She has a cold. We'll need to keep an eye on her tonight. If the fever's not gone by tomorrow, I'll take her to the doctor. You did the right thing by calling me, Liselle."

Liselle stared down at Ruby. The child cooed softly and snuggled close to her.

"Looks like you've made a friend," Aunt Zoe smiled. "Why don't you put her in her crib? I think she's ready."

Liselle walked slowly to Shayna's bedroom and gently placed Ruby in her crib. She was amazed at how helpless and lovely Ruby looked, resting peacefully in her nest of blankets and stuffed animals. Liselle let her hand drift over her own belly.

"You're a good girl," she whispered, kissing Ruby's forehead. "Everything's okay now."

When she returned to the living room, Aunt Zoe took Liselle by the shoulders. Liselle cringed, waiting for her aunt to yell at her, to shake Liselle like Dad did in her nightmare. But instead, Aunt Zoe gently kissed her forehead, just as Liselle had kissed Ruby. "You're a natural," she whispered.

Tears filled Liselle's eyes. "No, I'm not," she choked, unable to hold back the emotion that was building inside of her. All week she had been pretending that it wasn't a big deal to be pregnant, that someone—Dad, Shayna, Oscar—would make everything all right. But she couldn't pretend anymore. Just a few hours alone with Ruby had made the truth undeniable. Having a child was a huge responsibility. And Liselle wasn't sure she could handle it.

She buried her face in Aunt Zoe's shoulder, letting the tears stream down her face. "I was so scared tonight. She just kept crying and looking at me as if she wanted help. But I couldn't help her."

Liselle swallowed hard and continued, "What am I gonna do when *my* baby gets here? Dad . . . he thinks I should give it away."

"Well, this is *your* baby and *your* decision, not your father's, Liselle. With all due respect, your father has been hiding from his responsibilities for years. Maybe he's not the one who should be telling you how to handle yours," Aunt Zoe replied, her voice firm yet gentle.

"But maybe he's right," Liselle sobbed. "I don't know if I can do this, Aunt Zoe. I don't know what to do."

Aunt Zoe gathered Liselle into her broad arms. "You know, when you were a little girl, your mother and I took you to the mall to see Santa. Some of the kids were scared, but not you. You just walked right up to him and plopped yourself in his lap. And when he asked you if you'd been a good girl, you arched your little eyebrow and said, "You're *Santa*. Shouldn't you *know* that already?"

"Your mom and I, we just laughed and laughed," Aunt Zoe continued. "We couldn't believe how brave you were. How smart! How feisty!"

Liselle let out a small laugh, despite the tears still streaming from her eyes. "I remember. He didn't know what to say to me."

"Adoption is a brave choice to make," Aunt Zoe continued, her voice soft and loving. "And it's certainly something to think about. But if you decide to keep your child, I know you'll do a *terrific* job. I have no doubt."

"How do you know that?" Liselle asked. "I mean, I don't think I could just give it away, but I don't know how to be a mom, either."

"None of us did at first," Aunt Zoe replied with a smile. "I'm not gonna lie to you, Liselle. It's not easy. It's gonna change your world more than you know. But you just survived your first night alone with a baby. That's the hardest night of all. And the rest? You'll learn. You'll make a lot of mistakes along the way, I promise you that. But you're not alone. You have people in your life to help you along the way."

"Like who?" Liselle pleaded. *My father? Oscar? Shayna?*

"Like me, for one. And your mother, Liselle. You have your mother." Liselle tried to avoid her gaze, but Aunt Zoe pulled her close. "Sweetheart," she said softly, "don't you think it's time to go home?"

Home. The word seemed to wrap itself around Liselle, like Aunt Zoe's strong motherly arms.

"But me and Shayna," Liselle said, her voice weak and shaky. "We were gonna move in together."

"Do you really think that's a good idea?" Aunt Zoe sat wearily on the couch and rubbed her forehead, as if she was getting a headache. Her voice turned serious and sad. "You know, she was only seventeen when she had Ruby. She was a popular girl with lots of friends— more than I ever had at her age.

"She had no idea how her life would change after Ruby was born. I tried to warn her, I tried to prepare her. Ruby was a difficult infant. She had colic for six weeks. She just cried and cried, and it didn't matter what we did. We were all exhausted. A few of Shayna's friends came by, but they never stayed long. Most of them don't call anymore."

Liselle blushed at her aunt's words. *I stopped coming over, too,* she thought.

"It's not Ruby's fault that Shayna wants her old life back," Aunt Zoe continued, her voice frustrated and somber. "I love my daughter, but she's no kind of mother right now. I pray she comes to her senses and realizes that Ruby needs her. But until that day, it's my job to take care of that little girl. And I'll protect her with everything I got.

"Shayna isn't getting an apartment," Aunt Zoe added. "She isn't going anywhere. She hasn't had a job in months. And frankly, I don't think she could handle living on her own for two days."

Liselle stared at her aunt and tried to take in all that she was saying. She looked exhausted and so much older than the spry woman Liselle remembered as a child. Liselle suddenly thought about how angry, how scared, Mom had been when she found out Liselle was pregnant.

Mom thinks she's gonna have to raise my baby, Liselle thought. *Why wouldn't she, with the way I've been acting?* The past four months suddenly flashed before Liselle's eyes.

Sleeping with Oscar just to keep his attention.

Being too scared to go to the drug store herself.

Ignoring the signs her body was giving her.

Refusing to eat. Running away. Ditching school.

Maybe Mom's glad I'm gone, Liselle thought. *Maybe she doesn't want to end up like Aunt Zoe.*

"It's late," Aunt Zoe said. "Why don't you get some rest? In the morning, we'll call your mother."

"Maybe Mom doesn't want me to come home," Liselle said. "I've been here for a week. She hasn't tried to find me. She doesn't even know where I am."

To her surprise, Aunt Zoe began to laugh. "Oh sweetheart," she said with tender amusement, "Do you really think she'd just let you wander the streets?

She knows exactly where you are. She called me before you even got here. She wanted to come get you, but I convinced her to let you stay for a few days. I thought it might do you some good."

Suddenly, Shayna walked through the front door, her red jacket clutched in her hand. She froze as soon as she saw Aunt Zoe. Then she flashed Liselle an angry, accusing glare.

Liselle retreated to the bedroom. She checked on Ruby, who was curled in her blanket. Her forehead still felt warm, but she was resting peacefully. Aunt Zoe and Shayna argued in the living room, their tense voices echoing through the walls. After several minutes, Shayna came in and peered into the crib.

"Is she okay?" she asked, her voice defensive.

Liselle ignored her and gently rubbed Ruby's back. She could feel Shayna staring at her in the dimly lit room.

"I didn't know she was sick," she continued, her voice wavering slightly. "I wasn't gone *that* long." Shayna sniffed and wiped her eyes. Liselle didn't look at her. Her hands trembled.

"Sorry, all right?" Shayna grumbled. "Dang."

Shayna kept staring at her, as if she was waiting for Liselle to forgive her, to say *It's cool, girl. Ain't no big thing.* But Liselle said nothing. She glared at her cousin and shook her head angrily. *I looked up to you,* Liselle thought. *I used to follow you around when we were kids.*

Shayna's eyes suddenly flashed with anger. "Don't you judge me," she hissed. "You got no idea what's comin' for you. You'll see."

Liselle lay down on the stiff air mattress and turned away from Shayna. "I don't want to live with you anymore," she said. "I'll be gone tomorrow."

For several minutes, the room was quiet except for Ruby's soft breathing and the sounds of Shayna sniffling. She could feel Shayna's eyes burning into her. Liselle shivered, afraid to turn around.

"When we were little, I *hated* sleeping at your house," Shayna hissed into the dark room. "My friends thought you looked like a boy."

Liselle winced, as if she had been hit in the face. She pulled the blanket tight around her neck and pretended to be asleep.

"You were always a loser," Shayna

continued, choking back tears. "Now you're just a loser with a baby."

Liselle closed her eyes tight and pretended to be asleep, but for what felt like a very long time, Shayna's voice echoed in the darkness.

"You'll see," she wept. "You'll see."

Chapter 9

On Friday morning Liselle woke up early and packed her bag. She swallowed down one of the large purple vitamins the doctor had given her, and then checked on Ruby one last time before heading out.

The sky was clear, and a smoky mist rose up from the pavement. She felt guilty for leaving before Aunt Zoe woke up. *I just need one more day*, she thought to herself. *Just one more.*

She bought a large breakfast with the twenty dollars Brian had given her. Then she wandered through her old neighborhood, passing the rusty swingset where she used to play as a little girl and the bus stop where she had waited with Mom on her first day of elementary school. She walked by her father's apartment building and gazed up at his window. She peered through the doorway of Jackson's Diner, where Mom hurried from table to table.

Then she sat on a bench just a few blocks away from Bluford High and waited.

On Friday afternoon at 2:47 p.m., the gray metal doors of Bluford High School flung open. A stream of students flowed into the sunny parking lot, talking and laughing and bustling with energy.

Liselle Mason stood alone on the sidewalk, keeping a close eye on the crowd. At her feet lay her battered pink bag. Her white sneakers were mud-splattered from crossing Bluford's soggy football field, her baggy sweats brown at the bottom. Her once-neat cornrows were fuzzy and unraveling. She looked as if she had just rolled out of bed. A group of freshmen giggled as they passed her.

"That girl looks busted," a boy snickered.

Liselle didn't care how she looked. She scanned the sea of faces, searching for Oscar. Her heart thumped anxiously in her chest.

Liselle spotted Monique walking toward her.

"Liselle?" she said, arching her eyebrow in confusion. "Where have you *been*? I've been calling you all week." Monique looked her over. "What happened to you? You look like you been through a war or something."

"I have," she replied, looking past her friend. "You seen Oscar?"

Monique stared at her. "Yeah, he's around here somewhere. Why haven't you been in school? Last time I saw you, you were passing out in the cafeteria, and now you show up lookin' all homeless. I thought I saw your mom in Ms. Spencer's office on Monday. What's going *on*?"

"It's a long story," Liselle replied. "Listen, I really can't talk right now. I gotta find Oscar."

"You still chasin' after him? No offense, girl, but if you tryin' to get Oscar's attention, maybe you should've worn somethin' nicer. Speaking of which, I heard Lisa's havin' some people over tonight if you wanna . . ."

"Monique," Liselle said sharply, "I'm pregnant, okay? So no, I really don't wanna go to Lisa's."

Liselle searched through the sea of faces, young freshmen who still ran after each other like little kids, seniors who swaggered slowly. Finally she spotted Oscar's black jacket. He was walking with a group of boys. Jamil led the pack, talking loudly. They were all smiling except for Oscar, who lagged behind them and stared at the muddy ground.

"Pregnant?" Monique whispered. "But . . ."

Liselle took a deep breath, her eyes fixed. "Oscar!" she yelled.

"But we were gonna work at the mall this summer," Monique murmured.

"Oscar!" Liselle hollered again. "Over here." Oscar froze when he saw her. Liselle grabbed her bag and strode over to him, her back straight, her eyes steady and determined.

"We need to talk," she said firmly.

Oscar shoved his hands in his pockets and looked around nervously. "I was gonna call you," he insisted. Oscar glanced at her messy hair, then at his friends, who were waiting for him. "I'll call you later, all right?" Then, after a moment, "I swear."

Liselle shook her head. "You're lying. You're not gonna call me later. So we need to talk right now."

Oscar crossed his arms. "Fine," he grumbled. "What?"

"I need to know where you stand." Liselle swallowed hard. "I need to know what you're gonna do."

"What'd you mean?" Oscar shrugged. "I'll do whatever, I guess."

"Look," Liselle sighed, "I've learned a lot this week. I still got a lot to learn, but . . . I'm gonna need your help, Oscar. We're gonna need money. And diapers. And a crib. And a thermometer that you stick under their arm because babies get fevers. We're gonna need jobs, too. We gotta figure out how we're gonna take care of this baby. We can't act like kids anymore. We gotta grow up."

"I know," Oscar grumbled, rubbing his head.

"I know you don't like me," Liselle continued. "Maybe I don't like you much, either. I know we didn't mean for this to happen. But it *did*. It's happening right now. So, are you gonna help me? Tell me the truth."

Liselle's voice was rising. Several students looked over at them.

"Everything cool, bro?" shouted one of Oscar's friends.

"Yeah," he shouted back. Oscar leaned close to her. "What you want me to say, Liselle?" he whispered, his voice a mixture of impatience and fear. "I mean, I don't know what I'm supposed to do. It's not like I wanted this to happen. I'm only sixteen. I just moved here."

"I'm sixteen, too!" Liselle snapped. "It's not like *I* wanted this to happen!"

Liselle tried to fight the warm tears gathering in her eyes. A small crowd was forming around them. Kendra, the girl who had found Liselle in the bathroom just a week ago, looked on with concern.

Liselle tried to keep her voice steady. "Kids *need* a father. Tell me you know that. Tell me you ain't gonna just disappear."

"Oh no, not this chick again," Jamil said as he strode over and flung a protective arm around Oscar. Jamil chuckled when he saw her. She held his gaze and glared back.

"I remember you," he said with a smirk. "Oscar told me about you. You that crazy chick who won't leave him alone."

"Liselle, c'mon," Monique pleaded, grabbing her by the elbow. "Everybody's lookin' at us. Let's just get outta here."

"Yo Jamil, chill out bro," Oscar said,

his voice limp.

But Liselle didn't budge. "I ain't talkin' to you," she snapped at Jamil. Then she glared at Oscar. "You gonna say something? Or you just gonna let your stupid cousin talk for you as usual?"

"Whatcha just call me?" Jamil challenged, taking a step toward her.

"I said *stupid*," Liselle repeated, looking Jamil dead in his eye. "Are you *deaf* too? Should I talk slower?"

Liselle could barely contain the anger boiling within her. Laughter rippled through the crowd. Jamil's eyes flashed with rage.

"I know your game, girl," he hissed. "You got some kinda psycho crush on my cousin here. First you was a stalker, and now you makin' up stories." Jamil looked around at the sea of faces watching him. "Sayin' you're *pregnant*."

Several people gasped.

"Jamil, you need to back up!" Kendra stepped out of the crowd and pushed a sharp finger into Jamil's chest. "And the rest of y'all need to mind your business!"

"This ain't my fault!" Oscar suddenly blurted. "You're the one who came over *my* house. What did you expect? For me to be all happy? Maybe I don't *wanna* deal with all this."

"Yeah," Jamil growled. "From what I heard, you practically threw yourself at him." Jamil glanced around him. "I mean, how's he even supposed to know it's his?"

For a moment, the world went quiet. Liselle felt her legs buckle as if someone had kicked her. She couldn't hear the voices surrounding her, the cries that rose up at Jamil's words. Laughter. Angry shouts. Kendra pushing against Jamil's broad chest. Oscar wincing, hanging his head in shame.

Liselle knew she was screaming at him, but she couldn't hear her own voice. Only Oscar's face was clear to her in the crowd. Oscar, the boy she had met at a party just four months ago, who now looked like a little kid, scared and full of confusion. Liselle kept screaming, a sound of rage and fury, until Oscar turned away and ran across the slick, muddy field of Bluford High School.

"Security's comin'!" someone yelled.

Liselle felt a warm hand grab hers. Then she was running too. Hot salty tears streamed down her face as the high school disappeared behind her. Finally she heard an urgent voice next to her.

"Stop!" it said. "Liselle, just calm down. It's okay."

Kendra was standing next to her, panting and holding Liselle's pink bag.

"Are you all right?" she asked.

Liselle stared at her, unsure what to say. Her ears were ringing and deep in her chest she felt as if something had torn open. Like her heart had been ripped. "No. I'm not," she admitted.

"You wanna sit down or something?"

Liselle shook her head. "I gotta go. I got a doctor's appointment."

"I'm sorry about Jamil. That boy's a dog." Kendra looked at her thoughtfully. "That other kid, he's the father?"

Liselle nodded, unable to stop the tears that welled in her eyes. "He just stood there. Looking at the ground. Doing nothing."

"Maybe he's just scared," Kendra offered. "He'll come around. He just needs time, that's all."

"I don't think so," Liselle sniffed. "I don't think he has it in him. He ran away."

Liselle massaged her temples and looked at Kendra. "What was I screaming at him?"

"I don't know," Kendra said with a

smile. "I was too busy yellin' at Jamil. But whatever you said, that boy ran away like he wanted his momma. I ain't never seen a boy run so fast."

Kendra looked at her with pride. "You're fierce. I feel bad for anyone who tries to mess with you. Or your kid."

For a moment, the girls were quiet. "You got someone to go with you to the doctor? I'll go with you, if you want."

"Nah, it's okay," Liselle replied, staring at this girl she barely knew. "Thanks. For defending me back there. You didn't have to do that."

"Yeah I did," Kendra said, her voice firm. "I might not know you, but I know your situation. There's no way I'd stand by and let those boys talk to you that way."

Liselle wiped her eyes. She wondered where Monique had disappeared to. Kendra was the kind of person Liselle made fun of. She was smart, she worked in the principal's office, she stayed late after school to study. Now Liselle wondered if Kendra was the kind of person she should've been hanging out with all along.

"I should go," she said sadly, taking her soggy bag. "I got a lot to figure out."

"Okay," Kendra sighed, turning to

leave. "I'll see you around, I guess."

"Wait!" Liselle called out. "I haven't been in school for a week. And with the baby coming, I'm gonna need help. Studying and all. I've never been very good at school. Maybe you could help me," Liselle shrugged. "I mean, if you wanted . . ."

"Yeah, I'll help you," Kendra replied with a smile, "At least till I leave. I'm going away in September." For a moment, she was quiet. "I'm going to college," she said softly.

Of course you are, Liselle thought as she walked alone down the empty block. *Of course you are.*

It was 4:00 p.m. when Liselle Mason walked into the Brown Street Women's Health Clinic. Behind the front desk, an older woman smiled at her.

"Can I help you?" she asked warmly.

Liselle took a deep breath. "My name's Liselle Mason. I'm pregnant. I'm here to see the doctor."

The woman handed Liselle a clipboard with several sheets of paper. "I just need you to fill out these forms," she said.

Liselle stared at the long list of

questions. *How many weeks into your pregnancy? Describe your medical history in detail. Do you have any questions for the doctor today? Do you have any concerns about your pregnancy?*

"I don't know," Liselle murmured, looking at the woman. "I don't know the answers."

"Is there anyone here with you today?" the woman replied. "Someone to help you?"

Liselle hung her head. She tried to answer, but the words stuck in her throat. *No. I'm all alone.*

"Wait," Liselle said, pulling out her cell phone. "Maybe. Just gimme a minute." Liselle quickly dialed a phone number and waited. Then she heard a phone ring just behind her.

"I'm already here," said a familiar voice. "I'm right here."

Liselle turned. "Mom," she whispered, her eyes suddenly glistening. "I was just calling you."

Chapter 10

Four years later . . .

The Bluford High School library was silent.

Liselle leaned back heavily in her chair and looked at the students all around her. Some hung their heads, as if drained from hearing her story. Others stared up at her eagerly, as if waiting for the next sentence.

"I wish I could tell you that everything worked out. I wish I could say it was easy taking care of a baby," she continued. "Or that Mom didn't have to pick up an extra shift at the diner to pay for all the stuff we needed. I wish I could tell you Dad helped out more, and gave us money to pay for the doctor visits."

Liselle shook her head and laughed

to herself.

"I wish I could tell you on that hot summer night in June, when Kelena was born, I wasn't scared out of my mind, that I didn't scream in pain with the contractions. Or that Oscar showed up at the hospital and held my hand the whole time. Or that Kendra became my best friend. But I'm not gonna lie to you. This ain't a movie. And it sure ain't a love story."

Liselle had talked for more than an hour. She felt tired, older somehow, but also relieved. For the past four years, she tried not to think too much about Oscar, though he came around from time to time. She had seen Shayna a few times, but things were still tense, though they never talked about it. Maybe they would one day. But now, as she looked out at the room full of girls, she saw herself in every single one of them.

Will one of them end up like me? Liselle wondered, looking into their eyes. *Will one make the same mistakes I did?* She knew the answer. It was the reason Ms. Spencer wanted her to speak to them.

Yes.

The thought made Liselle wince. She

wanted to reach out and help these girls—to show them another way, to convince them to wait and finish school before they have a baby. Liselle leaned forward in her seat, her heart beginning to pound.

"What do you want to be when you grow up?" she asked, her voice suddenly strong and clear. "You!" she said, pointing to Jamee. "What do you want to be?"

"I don't know," Jamee answered nervously. "You mean, like, what kinda job do I want?"

"Yeah," Liselle pressed. "What do you dream about? What are you good at?"

"I don't know. I like music a lot, I guess," Jamee said quietly. "A producer maybe? Like one of those people who makes music videos."

"That sounds like a great job," Liselle grinned. "What about you?" she said, pointing to another girl at the back of the classroom. "What are you good at?"

"I like to cook," she said shyly.

"So maybe you want to be a chef. Like at one of those fancy restaurants downtown with the guys who park your car."

The girl smiled and looked down.

"You could even end up with your

own TV show," Liselle added with a wink. Laughter rippled through the room.

"Who else?" Liselle asked, surprised at how alive, how energetic she felt. "C'mon, just shout out your dreams. What do you want to be?"

The girls shifted in their seats and glanced at each other.

"I wanna be a fashion designer, maybe have my own store one day!" shouted Danisha, the round-faced girl.

"Great! Who else?"

Tamara, the girl whose phone Liselle had taken earlier, rolled her eyes. Her friend April was staring at the ground. She looked lost in thought.

"What about you?" Liselle asked April. "What are you good at?"

April shook her head slowly. "Nothing," she said simply, without looking up. "I'm not good at anything."

"That ain't true," Tamara laughed. "You're real good at failing all your tests. Yo, can she get a job doing that?"

"You should be a lawyer, Tamara," Liselle replied, raising her eyebrow. "You sure are good at interrupting people. I bet you could argue all day long."

The class erupted into laughter. Even

Tamara smiled, though she quickly tried to hide it. "A *lawyer*," Liselle heard her say under her breath.

"Yo, Ms. Mason," called out a girl from the back of the room. "What does this have to do with anything? I mean, so Jamee wants to make music videos. So what?"

Liselle smiled. "The point is, none of you said, 'I want to be a teenage mom.'"

The group grew silent. Eyes widened. Ms. Spencer nodded.

"Let me tell you how it is for me now," Liselle continued, her voice serious. "I wake up at 6:00 a.m. and shower, then eat a quick bowl of cereal. Kelena wakes up at 6:30. I change her, feed her, and take her to daycare. Then I go to work at the diner. On my feet, all day long. If I'm lucky, I get off work by 6:30 p.m., just in time to put Kelena to bed. Then I go to school for night class."

"I miss things," Liselle admitted, her voice softening, as if she was telling the class a secret. "Staying up late. Sleeping in. Doing nothing. Sometimes at night, I wish I could sneak out for a few hours, just to get a break, be by myself for a little while. On nights like those, I think about my cousin Shayna. She was right:

I had no idea what it was like to have a kid. But now I do, and though I get how she feels, I still stay home. Kelena needs me. It's not her fault if I have regrets."

"What about Oscar?" asked Danisha. "Did you ever hear from him again?"

"Not for a long time," Liselle replied. "But then, last year, he called me. At first I'd only let him meet us in a park or somewhere public. I didn't trust him. I still don't—not completely. But now he comes by once in a while. I can tell he's still nervous around Kelena. He's not sure what to do with her. But at least he's trying. That's something, I guess.

"But no matter what he does, *I'm* the one raising a four-year-old daughter every day. *I'm* the one fighting to stay awake in my classes each night. *I'm* the one struggling to pay for my textbooks each semester. Because of the choices I made, *I'm* the one who has to work a lot harder to reach my goals now.

"Having a baby . . ." Liselle's voice trailed off for a moment. "It's hard. I love Kelena. I love her more than any-thing. But it would've been nice to stay young. Just for a little bit longer. You hear me?"

The room was silent. Liselle could

feel the eyes focused on her.

"You girls," she said, her voice rising. "You can be *anything*. Producer. Designer. Chef. You're all so smart. But you need to be *relentless* too. Be *relentless* about your dreams. Be *relentless* about the kind of life you want to have. And don't let anything stand in your way. Not boys. Not sex. Nothing."

"Dang," Tamara murmured. "That's real, yo."

Liselle sighed and looked at Ms. Spencer. "I don't know what else to say," she admitted.

Ms. Spencer smiled, her eyes shining with pride. "What do *you* want to be, Liselle? You said you were taking classes. What do you plan on studying?"

"Me?" she replied, suddenly feeling a bit shy. "I'm not sure yet. I'm just takin' basic courses right now."

"You should be a teacher," Danisha blurted with a wide grin.

Several girls nodded in agreement. "Yeah," she heard someone whisper. "That girl speaks the truth."

"Nah," said Jamee. "She should be one of those people who talks to kids about their problems. Like a teacher, but you know, more personal."

"A counselor," Ms. Spencer nodded. "Absolutely."

Liselle blushed, amazed at how good, how proud she suddenly felt. When she had first returned to Bluford High School, she wondered if she had made a mistake. But now she felt her struggles might have a purpose, that maybe these girls were it.

Counselor, Liselle thought after the discussion ended, and the group of girls stood and clapped for her. *That's not a bad idea.*

Ms. Spencer dismissed everyone, and Liselle rushed to the girl's bathroom and changed into her Jackson's Diner uniform.

Counselor, she thought again, inspecting herself in the mirror one last time.

Counselor.

Just then the heavy metal door of the bathroom squealed open.

"Ms. Mason?" said a soft voice. April stood in the doorway, her face a mixture of fear and sadness. Her eyes glistened with tears.

"April? Are you okay?"

She hung her head, her hair falling around her face like a shroud. She sniffed and wiped her nose.

"I'm in trouble," she whispered. "I don't know what to do."

"Okay," said Liselle, gathering the girl into her arms. "I'm right here. Talk to me."

WELCOME TO BLUFORD HIGH.

IT'S NOT JUST SCHOOL—

IT'S REAL LIFE.